Santa Is Going Down On Me

Also by Marie Lipscomb

Romance books with plus-sized heroes and heroines.

The Hearts of Blackmere series:

The Lady's Champion

The Champion's Desire

Forever His Champion

The Vixens Rock series:

Rhythm

Strings

Amped

No Getting Ogre You (by Marie Lipscomb writing as M.L. Eliza)

Santa Claus is Going to Town On Me

Marie Lipscomb

writing as

M.L. Eliza

SANTA CLAUS IS GOING TO TOWN ON ME

Copyright © 2021 by M.L Eliza/Marie Lipscomb

Cover by Marie Lipscomb

All rights reserved.

No part of this book may be reproduced in any form or by any electronic or mechanical means, including information storage and retrieval systems, without written permission from the author, except for the use of brief quotations in a book review.

Fuck it, this one's for me.

I've always hated Christmas, but this year will be different, because this year,

I'm going to fuck Santa Claus.

CHAPTER ONE

Christmas can kiss my ass.

As I stalk down my upstairs hallway, my heart is beating out of my chest. It's Christmas Eve, I'm freezing-fricking-cold in my little red plaid pajama shorts, and I'm starting to wonder if a replica medieval broadsword was the best form of self-defense I could have grabbed. Knowing my luck, I'll swing and miss, and probably get the blade stuck in the wall. Great.

But the fucker is walking around downstairs, sneaking around in the dark, chuckling to himself, and rustling through the meagre pile of presents beneath my tree. I can't just do nothing.

I've lived alone for five years, dealt with hitherto untold heaps of bullshit, but this is my first time getting burgled. And, incidentally, it's going to be my first time murdering some dude with a sword.

"Fuck," I whisper, tightening my grip around the hilt. Silver moonlight streams through the hallway window, lengthening my shadow as I creep closer toward the top of the stairs. What I lack in height, I make up for in thickness. I'm fairly confident that if I tackle the guy, I can sit on him until the cops show, but that's only going to work if I can surprise him and knock him off balance. And if that doesn't work, then he's getting an ass-full of Mr. Stabbity.

Tiptoeing down the stairs, I'm just about blacking out from fear and stress. Waves of heat crash over me, my vision tilts and blurs.

I hate this.

Hate this asinine holiday. I hate that my parents named me Holly, so everyone just assumes I love Christmas. I hate the same sentimental movies shown every year, I hate jingle bells, I hate waking up on Christmas morning knowing I'm going to spend the day being asked why I'm still single at thirty-four. And most of all, I hate that I now feel unsafe in my own home.

Well, this guy is going to regret this night for the rest of his miserable life. All ten seconds he has left of it.

At the bottom of the stairs, I take a moment to steady my nerves. His footsteps are heavy and lumbering, thudding on my threadbare carpets. He sounds big and he isn't going anywhere in a hurry.

Holy shit. Holy shit.

I remind myself that the bigger they are, the harder they fall. He isn't expecting me, and that gives me something of an advantage. I hope.

God, I hope so.

I close my eyes and pull in a deep breath and hope it isn't my last. My fingers curl tight around the leather-wrapped hilt of the blade. This is it. I'm going in.

"Fuck you, asshole!" I scream as I leap around the corner and into my living room.

My vision fills with blurring multi-colored fairy lights, sparkling tinsel, and the biggest man I've ever seen. I stop, frozen in place.

It isn't his size that freezes me.

It isn't the fact he seems to be adding presents to the small pile beneath my tree, or that he's completely undaunted by me running at him with a replica sword.

No.

It's the big red coat, the big black boots, the luxurious white plush of his beard. It's the way his eyes rake over me, starting at my ankles, tracing the bare length of my legs, my thighs, and up and up until he reaches my eyes. My pajamas aren't the most modest, but by the time he's done with me, I feel stripped bare.

"Are…" I feel so ridiculous as I lower my blade. My chest is heaving. "You look like—You can't be—"

He sets a box down beneath my tree, and turns to face me. He has to be at least seven feet tall, and so broad he would have to tuck in his big, bulky arms to get through the front door. A thick, dark grey eyebrow arches as he waits for me to regain some semblance of eloquence.

But I can't finish my sentence. I can't say what he looks like, because it's absurd. He isn't real. He can't be real. Even as a kid I knew it was all pretend.

And yet…

I can't take my eyes off him as he shoves one of his enormous hands into the pocket of his thick red coat and pulls out a scroll of paper. Not paper, parchment, like something a wizard would write on.

As if by magic it unfurls in his hands. He puts on a pair of half-moon, gold-rimmed glasses, and peers at me above them. My breath catches, and the gentle, barely perceptible tingles in my belly begin to roll through me. Specifically, downwards.

God, he's a stern Christmas daddy.

"Holly?" His voice is deep, but soft and gentle.

"Yeah?" I reply.

He frowns. "Holly Parson?"

"No..." This isn't happening. This is not happening! "Holly Pearson."

"Ah, shoot. Wrong house."

Laughter bursts from me. I let my sword rest against the wall and take a nervous step toward him. "Are you—? Are you really Santa?"

"Yes." There's a darkness in his voice now. The softness is gone, replaced by something more primal. He smells manly; like smoke, leather, and wood shavings.

I'm certain he hasn't climbed down my chimney, because the flue for my wood burning stove is only about seven inches in diameter. I attempt to collect myself. "You're real?"

His moustache quirks as he smiles and pats his broad, thick torso, as if making sure he has a solid form. "Last I checked."

My head is swimming. Not only is Santa real, not only is he casually standing in my living room after I charged at him wielding a sword… he's also HOT. He has an accent I can't place, sort of European but not like anything I've heard before. All I know is that I dig it.

His eyes meet mine, and I can't turn away. They're absurdly vivid sapphire blue, the same blue as a crisp winter night sky. I've never seen eyes like them. His nose is quite large and he has a definite kink in the middle, as though it has been broken and reset slightly wrong. I'd always thought Santa was supposed to be a jolly old man, but he doesn't appear to be old or jolly at all, other than the big white beard and the soft curls of white hair beneath his hat. But he doesn't look young either. He's sort of… ageless, I guess. In any case, he's gorgeous.

"I'm sorry," he says, his voice just a throaty whisper. "I must have got the addresses mixed up. I didn't mean to startle you."

"Hmm?"

Shit. I snap back to the room and realize I was staring at him with full-blown heart eyes. Turning back toward the tree, I try to regroup. A small pile of presents, perfectly wrapped in immaculate red wrapping paper and topped with golden bows, lie by my feet. They're easy to distinguish from my lumpy silver snowflake paper wrapped monstrosities. Each one of his gifts bears a golden tag, with the neatly written words, *To Holly, Merry Christmas, from Santa.*

For a moment, my heart flutters, but then I remember I'm the wrong Holly.

"I doubt you'd really want them anyway," he chuckles, as though he can read my mind. "The other Holly is five years old, and she's only interested in ponies and pots of slime that make farty noises when you poke them."

"Farty noises?"

"Apparently so. But she's a good kid, and I should get these gifts to her."

He kneels down and begins picking up the presents, placing them carefully in a big brown sack next to him.

"Oh my god," I hear myself whisper, even as I tell myself to chill. "Is that the sack?"

Another chuckle, another glance from his twinkling blue eyes, another round of flutters heading south. The apples of his cheeks grow rosy.

"Let me help," I say, dropping to my knees beside him.

"Thank you. This mishap has left me pretty far behind schedule."

"Can you catch up?"

His eyes narrow as he calculates something. "I'm about fifteen thousand houses behind."

"Fifteen thousand?"

He shrugs a massive shoulder and tightens the string fastening the sack. Of course, his arms and shoulders are big and strong.

They have to be to lug that huge sack of toys around. "I'll catch up. It's no problem. This isn't my first rodeo."

He's so confident, so self-assured, and I can't help but to wonder what it would be like—and I can't believe I'm actually thinking this—to fuck Santa Claus. And I want to, I realize. Desperately. I never wish for anything at Christmas anymore, but now, beneath my tree, I find myself wishing hard.

A longing breath leaves his lips as though he hears my thoughts. Can he read my mind?

"Look," he says, pulling himself to his feet with a strained groan. I stay on my knees in front of him, watching his cheeks redden. "I'm going to be honest with you. I know exactly what you want. Knowing your desires is one of my abilities."

Shit. Now it's my turn to blush. And just like that, my treacherous brain switches from vague wishes, to full-blown vivid fantasies. God, I want to straddle those wide hips, feel him thrust up into me, filling me. I want him. I need him. My pussy tingles and tightens, and I know I'm getting wet, kneeling before Santa Claus in front of my Christmas tree.

Ugh. Fuck this holiday, seriously. And also, hopefully, literally.

His big, broad chest swells above me, and his lips part beneath the soft, snowy mass of his beard.

"I'm sorry," I whisper, my voice thick and husky with desire. "I can't help thinking about it."

"I know. And I can't help but listen. I know you'd probably much rather keep those thoughts private, but I can't just turn it off."

But I don't want him to stop hearing me. I kind of like letting him know how sexy he is, and how much I desire him. And from the bulge swelling beneath the hem of his coat, I guess he likes it.

He sighs a little. "I'm sorry, Holly. I have to go."

Offering me a big, strong hand, he helps me up from the floor. Now that I'm standing, I'm sure he's shrunk a little. Though still tall, he's not quite as huge as he was before. He's just the right height for me to kiss if I was to stand on my tiptoes.

His eyebrows bunch as he effortlessly slings the cumbersome sack over his shoulder. "Are you… do you have plans tomorrow?"

"Um… yeah kinda. It's Christmas Day," I chuckle.

"Ah, yes. I forgot about that."

"You forgot Christmas Day?"

He laughs, a deep laugh which shakes his chest and belly. "I suppose I did. I'm more of a Christmas Eve kind of guy. And, in my defense, my head is currently filled with very unfestive thoughts. And believe me, not all of them are yours."

The desire to press myself against him buffets against my back, and I have to fight not to step toward him. I want him. I want all that man between my thighs.

"I should be home around six," I say.

He nods and pulls his bottom lip between his teeth. "I'll be here. If you still want me, that is."

"I will. I know I will."

He smiles. "Until tomorrow then."

It's driving me crazy. I just want a taste, just enough to get me through Christmas Day. I want him to kiss me, to take me now. Pull aside the flimsy crotch of my shorts and bend me over the couch.

There's an urgency in his eyes, a beastly hunger sending color flooding across his cheeks. As if in response my entire body floods with heat and I can't bear it anymore. I know he knows what I'm thinking; I desperately want Santa Claus to fuck me, take me, absolutely obliterate me.

But he doesn't.

Instead, he reaches out, and brushes one of his big, warm hands through my sleep-tousled hair, before letting it drift down to firmly grip my chin.

"I'll be back for you," he says, teasing the plump pillow of my lower lip with his thumb. "And when I do, I'll make sure the wait is worth it."

This… should be weird, but it doesn't feel wrong. It feels oh so right.

I want to suck his thumb into my mouth, tease it with my tongue and teeth, let him know what I intend to do to him tomorrow. He turns me on like no one I've ever met before. My nipples ache with the need to be touched, and my pussy pulses with the desire to have him.

"In good time," he tells me. He closes the space between us with a step, pressing his big body against mine.

Fuck, I'm so horny I'm lightheaded.

"Tomorrow, I'll give you everything you want, but tonight, I have a job to do. If I give in now, I don't think my whole team of reindeer could pull me away from you. And there will be a lot of very upset children tomorrow."

I nod. "I know." In fact, I know that sadness all too well.

A shudder of breath escapes me as he pulls away his hand, and I immediately miss the sensation of his touch, the warmth of his body.

There's agony in his eyes as he turns and heads toward the wood burning stove in the torn-out fireplace. "If I come back here tomorrow, and you have second thoughts, tell me and I'll go. I won't try to change your mind. But if you want me, then I'll be here, and you'll get everything you've ever wanted."

The thought of fucking someone who knows my every wish and desire makes my stomach flutter. Christmas Day always drags, but getting through tomorrow while waiting for him to come back will be absolute torture.

"I'll make it worth the wait, Holly," he smiles, as he stomps over to the stove. "And while you're touching yourself tonight, I want you to think of me."

The groan of the woodburner's iron door masks the sound of my breathless whimper. With a smirk he places one boot among the embers and I start to wonder if we've both completely lost our minds. But even as I begin to doubt, he disappears in a flash of brilliant white light. Silver snowflakes dust the top of the stove.

He's gone, but the heat raging through my body isn't. I stand there until the snowflakes melt, and though the logical, no-fun part of my brain tells me this can't actually be happening, my body remembers his presence all too vividly.

I lie in bed later that night, thoughts of him running through my mind. I'm too excited to sleep, and far, far too horny.

Every year since I was four, I've hated Christmas, but I know tomorrow will be different. Because tomorrow, I'm going to fuck Santa Claus.

CHAPTER TWO

I'm physically there for the gifts and the food and the Lampoons on TV, but mentally, I'm over three thousand miles away at the North Pole, bare-assed and sitting on Santa's lap. I hardly register my relatives' questions about my love life and my mom's tipsy comments about my dad. Normally those things would hurt, but today I'm just counting down the seconds before I get that Santa dick.

By five thirty I'm racing out the door of my mom's house, and by five minutes to six, my fingers are shaking as I unlock my own front door, wondering if I have enough time to shower before he jingles me all the way.

My heart skips a beat as an icy wind blows against my back, carrying a sparkling trail of silvery snow which leads from the front door to my Christmas tree. A single gift sits beneath my tree, wrapped in red paper and topped with a golden bow. I know it's him, even though I never got gifts from him as a child. I recognize the wrapping from last night. The knowledge he has been in my house without me should irk me, but he's Santa Claus. He gets a pass.

My body trembles as I approach, and it's hard not to let disappointment settle into my heart like a deep winter frost. Does this mean he isn't coming? Did he have second thoughts?

The box is light, and it smells kind of like him; smoke and leather, and just the slightest hint of gingerbread. There's a tag wedged beneath the bow, and flipping it over I read, "To Holly (the right one this time). Do you feel naughty or nice? Love, C."

Anticipation of what's inside scares me just as much as excites me, but I'm only going to live once. Let's fucking do this. Carefully, I unravel the bow, and slide my finger beneath the seam of the paper. It comes apart in my hands, revealing two flat boxes stacked one on top of the other. One sleek red, the other pure white.

My belly tightens. I know exactly which one I'm going for. I've spent all night and all day waiting for this, and right now, I'm feeling extremely naughty.

I carry both boxes up to my room and set the white one aside on my dresser. Placing the red one on my bed, my heart rate grows faster as I stare, wondering what he has left for me.

I can't take it anymore. I have to know.

Yanking the lid off the box, I'm greeted with a pile of soft red tissue paper and a dusting of glitter... no...it's snow. Real snow. Cold to the touch, but weirdly dry, and just as soon as it comes into contact with the warmth of my palm, it disappears. Magic.

Head swimming, I lift the tissue paper to find my gift.

"So, you felt naughty?" His voice rumbles in my ear, and his breath blows warm against my neck.

The box falls from my hands. I don't know how he got in here, or how such a large man can move so quietly and go completely undetected, but his presence sends electric tingles shooting through my body. The air fills with the scent of soot, and the warmth of his skin, and all I want to do is turn around and pounce on him.

"I thought about you all day." I can barely speak as he pulls back the curtain of my hair and begins to kiss my neck. All my thoughts are erased by the sensation of his soft, eager lips, the silky plush warmth of his beard against my sensitive skin.

"I know," he growls against my ear, sending a shiver through my body. "I slept as much as I could after last night, but every dream I had was of you. And I could still hear your wishes."

"Oh…" Sympathy knots my stomach. He has to be exhausted after visiting so many homes last night. He's travelled so far even just to get to me. I should offer to take a rain check on this, give him time to rest fully and…

"Don't even think it," he chuckles as he wraps his big, strong arms around me. "I travelled so far because I want you. And you're worth every centimeter of my journey"

I lean back into him, my breath snagging in my chest as he cups my breasts, and strokes his thumbs over my hardened nipples through the fabric of my dress. Fuck, he feels so good. "You're sure?"

And then he spins me, turns me around to face him. His white hair is brushed back, sleek, though the curls at the bottom brush the tops of his heavy shoulders. Last night he was dressed all in scarlet felt and white fur, today he's dressed in thick, burgundy wool. And blue denim jeans. I almost laugh. Santa wears blue jeans.

"I don't wear the uniform all the time," he smiles. His dark blue eyes still have that mischievous glint. "And, yes, I'm sure. I'm not tired. My stamina isn't like that of mortal men."

Ooh. I shiver at the boast. He's like a superhero then; mind reading powers, superhuman stamina, possible shapeshifting.

I step closer to him, and as I do, one of his hands trails down my back and stops on my waist, while he cups the other at the back of my neck, urging me closer still. I can't believe this is real.

He's still at that kissable height, just a few inches above me. All I have to do is stand on my tiptoes and push through the silk of his beard. He meets me halfway, stooping slightly to reach my lips, and for a moment I feel my soul leave my body. My whole world encompasses nothing more than him, his eager, demanding lips, the heat of his tongue teasing mine. I bite into his lower lip, feeling the throb between my thighs as he groans.

I wish he would just take me now. And just as soon as the thought enters my mind, he pushes against me, his thighs bumping mine as he takes a step, nudging me toward the bed.

This is happening. THIS IS HAPPENING.

The excitement makes me shiver. I don't even care what's in the box anymore. I just want him for a moment. No gimmicks, no fussy details to distract us. Just him, his lips all over me.

He pulls away from our kiss for just a moment, leaving behind a faint taste of hot cocoa on my lips. In one quick motion, he lifts his sweater over his head, and holy fuck…

Last night when I was stalking through my hallway with my sword, I felt like I would black out from the anxiety. But now, now I feel that same sensation, the blurring of my vision, the tightening of my chest, but it isn't fear. It's need.

His arms and shoulders are muscular and sturdy, but his stomach and the rest of his torso is big, round, and soft. Silver hairs gleam on his chest, and trail from his bellybutton, down to the waistband of his jeans. His nipples are puckered, dark pink peaks on the soft mounds of his chest. I knew he was a big dude. Hell, everyone who knows who Santa Claus is can generally agree that he's on the thicker end of the scale. He's absolutely my type. But I'm not prepared for just how big and burly, and downright sexy he is.

My hands have a mind of their own as I reach out, caressing the curves of his torso. He emanates so much heat. I crave him like I've never craved anything before.

He rushes back toward me as though he can't stand to be away from me, any more than I can stand another second of this distance. Splaying his fingers at the back of my head, he pulls me into a passionate, claiming kiss, and together we sink down onto the bed.

We lay side-by-side, kissing, touching, exploring each other's bodies. And all the while, anything I wish he grants. I crave the touch of his big, warm hands on my thighs, and instantly, he obliges, stroking my soft, dimpled skin there, reaching beneath my skirt to caress my ass. I want to be naked, to feel our bodies touch without barriers. As soon as I think it, I'm unwrapped as if by magic, my clothes falling away just like the paper on the present he left for me.

He grins at my startled gasp. The heat in my house is turned up pretty high, but as he laughs, a cold breeze seems to blow from nowhere, pebbling my skin and puckering my nipples.

"Are you doing that?" I ask.

He shrugs, feigning innocence, but the way his eyes keep drifting back to my tits gives him away. He's totally doing it on purpose and I love it.

The warmth and wetness of his mouth against my cold, hard nipples makes me gasp. The soft fluff of his beard brushes against my stomach, tickling and teasing and driving me wild. He sucks hard on my nipple, then pulls away, sticking his tongue out to lick them so that I can watch. Fuck, he's so sexy. And from the proud smirk he gives me as his white mane tumbles over his broad shoulders, he's well aware just how sexy he is.

Laying back, I hold his gaze, and silently wish his jeans away. But there's no magical unwrapping this time. Instead, he gets out of bed and stands, slowly unbuckling his belt, and then inching down his pants. I bite by lip as my chest flutters. Every depiction of Santa's underwear I've ever seen has him wearing those cartoon boxers with pink hearts all over them, but the reality is far more appealing. His boxer briefs are form-fitting, wine red, and stretched over his wide hips and bulging erection.

I squeeze my thighs together in anticipation. I can already feel the wetness between them, hot and slick and aching. He notices it too. His breathing stops, and his lips part as he drinks in the sight of me, the sight of my pussy laid bare by his magic. Those dark sapphire eyes turn black with desire.

"Holly," he whispers my name like a plea. "You're so beautiful."

I want those lips on my pussy. I want to feel his beard against my inner thighs. I want him. I want. I want.

And just like every want I've had so far, he's only too happy to oblige.

Slowly, on his hands and knees, he works his way toward me, his sapphire eyes fixed on my pussy, his lips parted in desperation. His wild hunger for me tightens knots in my stomach, and I can hardly catch my breath as he pulls my thighs wide and pins them with his strong hands, so my knees are almost at my chest. I'm completely exposed to him, completely at his mercy, and so desperate to feel his mouth on me. There will be time for foreplay later. Right now I'm wet and needy, and I want to feel him between my legs.

A light icy mist against my pussy draws a gasp from my lips. Mistletoe hangs in the air above us, and snow sprinkles down onto me.

I can't help but laugh. "You're so corny." But my laughter is cut short by the shock of the sensation of his tongue.

The first lick is slow, painfully, tormentingly slow. He drags his tongue along my folds, tasting every inch of me. I can't contain my cry, pressing my back into the mattress as I try to lift my hips and take more from him, try to charge headlong into my orgasm. But he has me pinned, and his Santa powers mean he knows that deep down, I want to be teased. He knows that deep down I want this to last all night.

"You taste so good," he says, his deep voice rumbling against my clit. But he doesn't touch me there, not yet.

He starts to kiss me, making out with my pussy, his tongue dipping into me, tasting all of me. Santa Claus is absolutely going to town on me, and I can't get enough of it. The cold of the snow, the heat of his mouth, it keeps me sensitive, as though each kiss is the first. He releases my legs and lets me rest my thighs on his sturdy shoulders, lets me tangle my fingers in his soft, white hair.

"Ho... ho... holy fuck," I gasp. I'm pretty sure he's going to have to peel me off the ceiling by the time he's done with me. My pleasure builds as my muscles clench around his tongue. If he keeps it up, I might come just from the sensation of his tongue slipping into me, but he has other plans.

I cry out in protest as he pulls out, and the chill of the snow against my pussy is torture. I go to close my legs, but he stops me, prying my knees apart with superhuman strength.

"Keep them open," he says. "I want to see you."

I can only nod, my nipples tightening still at the sound of the command, rumbling in his deep voice.

"Good. You said you were feeling naughty, but you didn't even look at your present."

I'd almost forgotten the scarlet box lying on the floor by the bed, but as he reaches for it, I'm desperate to know what's inside. The skin of my thighs rises into goosebumps, both from the anticipation and the cold of the feathery snow

The red tissue paper rustles as he takes it out of the box, revealing my gift. Mischief glimmers in his eyes as he unravels two long lengths of scarlet silk ribbon. My belly tightens at the thought of him tying me up, having me completely at his mercy.

The slow smile which lifts his lips is enough to let me know he heard my desires loud and clear. In the next heartbeat the ribbons have magically slipped under the mattress and their ends have bound my wrists and ankles, holding me spread-eagled and decorated with four immaculate bows.

My chest rises and falls sharply in anticipation of what he'll do next. The snow falls slowly all over my body, each flake like a soft, icy kiss.

Being tied up like a gift for Santa Claus is exciting enough, but something else is rolling around in the box too, and I can barely contain myself. He pulls out a candy cane striped thing and sits at the side of my hip, turning it over in his hands. It's flat and round, polka-dotted with white buttons. It looks sort of like a suction cup, but there's something jiggling around inside the "mouth" part of it.

"Did your elves make that?" I ask, half joking.

He chuckles. "I don't have elves. It's just me up there making all the toys. But I made this one especially for you."

"What does it do?" I'm trembling now, both afraid and aroused, and desperate to know what new sensation his magical mind has come up with for me.

This excitement almost makes up for all the years he passed over my house and didn't leave me anything.

With an arch of his eyebrow, the ribbons around my ankles tighten, spreading my legs wider. He slowly caresses the inside of my thigh and says, "I'll show you."

His teasing earlier has left me wet and desperate, and the gentle touch of his fingertips as he places the contraption over my clit almost makes me cry out. My breath stops as he kneels between my knees and hooks his thumbs beneath the waistband of his boxers. This is it. I'm going to see his Santa cock.

And what a cock he has. His shimmering silver bush gleams at me as his dick bobs free of its confines, hard and curved upward. It's thick, almost intimidatingly so, but my pussy tightens as though I can pull him inside me just by sheer force of will.

"Patience," he smiles, dragging a finger between my folds, coaxing a moan from my lips.

"I want you so bad, Santa."

"I know."

I lie completely still as he tinkers with the device covering my clit. It seems to be suctioned securely to me, and that in itself is a pleasant sensation. But then he turns it on, and I'm fairly sure the world could explode around me and I simply wouldn't give a shit.

It's almost exactly like his mouth, insatiable, warm and wet, licking and sucking my clit exactly how I want it. Long, savoring licks, light fluttering teases, ravenous sucks, keeping me on the edge of orgasm, but never letting me tip over into sheer bliss. And all I can do is lie there, gasping and moaning as he watches me, stroking his big hand along his length, beads of pre-cum glistening at the dark pink head of his cock.

"I love tasting you myself, but this way I get to watch you," he growls. "And I get to fuck you while you come again and again, all over my cock."

I can't tear my eyes from him as he rolls a condom over his erection. The sensation of the tongue circling my swollen clit, bringing me close and then backing off, has me sobbing. "Please…fuck me. Santa…"

"Claus," he says. The way he says it, it rhymes with house rather than claws. "Call me Claus. Everyone pronounces it wrong."

Anything he asks. "Claus, please. God, fuck me."

He smirks, stroking his length once more. "Naughty or nice?"

"Naughty," I pant. "Hard, fast, however you want, I don't care. Just fuck me. I need it."

It's clear he needs it too. The force with which he enters me tips me into an orgasm which rips through my body, almost lifting me from the bed as my pussy tightens and pulses around his cock. And then I realize that I am off the bed. I'm floating as he thrusts into me, weightless but still bound as his heavy balls slap against my ass cheeks. Of course he has a massive sack.

The device on my clit keeps licking, driving my waves of pleasure. I never want this to end. There's so much of him, so much I couldn't wrap my legs around him even if I could move them. And as I feel my next orgasm start to swell, I realize he's getting bigger.

Every part of him.

CHAPTER THREE

If this is how I die, then so be it. I'd consider the past ten minutes to be the best of my life. Claus grows as he fucks me–getting taller, wider, girthier, filling me, stretching me, and even though my neighbors live a while away, I don't doubt they can hear me cry out his name.

He thrusts into me as I float above the bed, his power and stamina unlike anything I've ever known, and all the while the toy he made just for me licks and sucks my clit, coaxing endless waves of pleasure. His big hands cup my tits, pinching my aching nipples between his fingers, just the slightest bit of pain to offset all this pleasure.

I don't know how many times I come. After the second time, the orgasms all roll through me, one after the other, barely giving me a moment to differentiate between them. I bite my lip as another spasm of pleasure tears through me, and my pussy grips his cock as if my life depends on it.

"I'm close," he whispers, his eyes screwed tight as his hands dig into my hips, pulling me onto him.

"Fuck, yes, Claus," I cry out through gritted teeth. "I want to feel you come."

My wish is his command. He groans, loud and deep as he thrusts into me one last time, his back arching, his fingertips digging into my hips. Weirdly, the air fills with the scent of peppermint. I don't have time to dwell on it though as my own body clenches, and a powerful orgasm builds inside me, swelling and tingling until it bursts, tearing through my body, a savage, unrelenting force.

I sob his name as my toes curl and my legs tremble until he collapses onto me, the silken softness of his hair and beard against my stomach. And just like that I'm back on the bed, free to move my arms and legs, the device detached and set aside on my bedside table.

I lie there, shellshocked, the world going on around me as if everything is normal, but I'm no longer part of it. I just had the best sex of my life—the best sex of anyone's life—with Santa Claus.

"Are you okay?" He asks gently, lying beside me, naked. His chest and belly are flushed pink like his cheeks. I'm completely spent, but just the sight of him all flustered and blushing like that is enough to give me a little twinge of need.

But I can't form words. I no longer remember how to function as a human being. I can only nod and curl onto my side, nestling against the warmth of his body as he strokes my back with his fingertips.

The next time I open my eyes, I feel as though I've been hit by a train... but, like, a really sexy one. My body aches, but I'm content and safe and cared for. I don't know or care how long I slept, only that he's still beside me, holding me, keeping me warm.

When he notices my eyes are open, he bends down to kiss my temple. "What do you need?"

"Just this," I murmur against his silver dusted chest. "You."

"You have me," he whispers.

My arm is heavy as I lift it and lay it over his hip, somewhat reciprocating his affection. It's all I can manage right now. "What are you?"

His chest rumbles with a deep chuckle. "I don't know."

"But you're not human…"

"No."

He's a conundrum is what he is. A mythical man who turned out to be real. A living, breathing being with superpowers and magic. And he's here, in my bed.

I press closer and kiss his chest, just above his heart. "I have so many questions."

"Ask them."

I can't ask them all. Some of them I'm afraid to know the answer to. Some of them I fear will put an end to all of this warmth and comfort. So, I start with the easy stuff.

"Do you really live at the North Pole? Is that what your accent is? A North Pole accent?"

"No."

His answer catches me off guard. I'm vaguely disappointed. "Oh."

"I lived there for a time, long ago, before people began to explore that part of the world. The mail services know to redirect the letters to my workshop."

"And where is that?"

He chuckles and strokes his hand along the curve of my cheek. "Far away."

Hm. Okay. That doesn't really answer my question, but I don't want to press him. "You said you don't actually have any elves?"

"No elves, no. I sometimes wish I did. It would definitely make things easier. And besides, I'd welcome the company."

His answer hurts more than I expect it to. Wherever he lives, it's remote enough that no one has ever found him, and that means it must get lonely.

"What about reindeer?"

His face brightens, and his cheeks grow round as he beams. "Of course, the reindeer are real. The sleigh can't pull itself.

Although, the ones you've heard of are long passed. But my current team is from the same herd."

I smile. That answers my next question too. The sleigh is real. One day, if this continues, I might ask him if I can ride on it, maybe see his workshop, but we're already hurtling into unknown territory, and I need to pull back the reins a little. "How old are you?"

He pulls in a deep breath. "Honestly, I don't know."

"Roughly?"

"I stopped counting at a thousand, and that was centuries ago."

Shit. I'm acutely aware of the earth's spinning. I was expecting him to say there had been different Santas through the ages, or that he was at most a couple of centuries old, but over a thousand?

He's known the world without electricity, a world where knights fought battles for kings and had real swords, not just replica ones. And now he's here, in bed with me. Just a little while ago he had his tongue in my pussy. I don't know whether this information should make me feel insignificant or vastly important. May as well settle on the latter.

"May I ask you some questions too?" He says gently.

I nod, overwhelmed by it all.

"Okay," he kisses my temple again, before wriggling down the bed to rest his head on the pillow beside me. I can smell myself on him, the scent of my arousal tangled with the scent of peppermint hot chocolate. His blue eyes flicker over my head as he glances at the wall. "First of all, why do you have a sword?"

Laughter bursts from me again. I know it's ridiculous. Less than twenty-four hours ago I was charging at him intent on skewering him on my museum quality replica broadsword, but now I'm wrapped in his arms, pressed against his big, warm body, his apparently permanently stiff cock pressing into my thigh.

He stares at me, waiting for a reasonable, logical explanation which I just can't give. So, I settle for the truth. "Because it looks cool."

His bushy grey eyebrows lift and he nods. "That's fair."

The smile which breaks across his face sends a flurry of tingles whirling through my belly.

"Next question," he says. There's hesitation in his voice, and I'm sure I hear a little nervousness. "I know you might not know the answer to this yet, and that's okay, but where do we go from here?"

He's asking me? The guy who stopped counting birthdays after a thousand, the superhuman mythical being lying next to me, is asking me what happens next. "I...I don't know."

"That's okay," he smiles. "If you want me to go, I'll go. If you want me to spend the night and cook you breakfast, I'll do it. Whatever you want from this, I'm willing to give."

What do I want? This all feels so lovely, so perfect. I feel like I've known him my whole life, and in a way I have. Against my better judgement I allow my imagination to leap ahead, trying to picture a future where Claus and I are together. How would I introduce this literal demigod to my mom? What would it be like walking down the high street hand-in-hand with one of the most instantly recognizable people in the world? Could we even do that? Would staying with him mean being locked away in a remote workshop, thousands of miles away from the world I know?

I can't think about it. All I know is that right here, right now, I feel good. He feels good. And for now, that's enough.

CHAPTER FOUR

I'm alone and naked when I wake up, but there's nothing unusual about that. I always wake up alone and I sometimes sleep without pajamas.

Blinking in the dull winter morning light, I reminisce about the incredibly vivid, incredibly weird sex dream I had about Santa Claus of all people. Sinking my teeth into my lower lip I stretch and yawn, and swear an oath never to tell anyone about it. Staying in bed today seems like a good plan. I must've been thrashing around in my sleep, because my body aches all over.

Reaching out toward the bedside table to grab my phone, I feel something weird. A curved object, covered in buttons... oh god.

My heart skips as I turn my head. The candy cane striped device rests on the table beside my bed. It was real. And that means he was real. But he seems to have left.

Perhaps it was just a one-night stand after all. I didn't give him an answer when he asked what I wanted to happen next, so maybe he took it as a hint and flew away.

I'm not sure how I feel about that.

Part of me is relieved I don't have to navigate a life in which I'm getting down and dirty with a beloved cryptid, but another (honestly, far larger) part of me is gutted. He didn't even say goodbye. I've always gotten too attached, always clung to people I find comfort in, and no one has comforted me like he has.

This kinda sucks.

But hey, at least he left me the toy.

Turning it over in my hands, I can't figure out how it works at all. None of the buttons are labeled, and he didn't exactly leave an instruction manual. It's compact and fits easily in the center of my palm. The concave underside is filled with some kind of bumpy, firm gelatinous substance. Last night it felt so much like a real mouth, warm and wet and eager to please me.

I wonder if it feels the same today.

He would want me to use it, I'm certain. He left it behind for a reason. I place it over my clit and it suctions on as if it has a mind of its own. No matter how I pull, I can't get it off. My heart kicks against my ribs, and I try not to panic. One of the buttons must release it so I start pressing them.

One of them has to... oh...oh.

The sensation of it licking me, fluttering its magical tongue against my clit makes me forget my worry as I lose myself to pleasure. It starts quickly, then laves me with slow, savoring arcs.

A moan escapes my lips as I sink back against the pillows and close my eyes, picturing him between my thighs, remembering the feeling of him thrusting into me as I floated, weightless and at his mercy. There was so much more I wanted to do with him, things I wanted to do to him. I picture him tied up on my bed, helpless as I tease and pleasure him, lavishing attention on every inch of that big, mystical body.

"Ah, you're awake." His deep voice sends a shock of panic through my chest. He stands in the doorway, holding a breakfast tray in his hands. There's orange juice, coffee, toast, and other things I can't quite make out.

Pulling the sheets up over my chest, I force a smile. The thing between my legs keeps licking me, demanding my orgasm, but

I'm too embarrassed to give in. He arches an eyebrow as if he knows, but he doesn't make a comment. Instead, he steps into the room and sets the tray on my dresser.

"Claus! I thought you'd left," I say, squeezing my thighs together to stave off the pleasure.

"No, I'm still here," he replies, confusion etched across his brow. "Unless you want me to go?"

I don't. I really don't. He looks so good this morning, wrapped in a big fluffy red bathrobe trimmed with white fleece. His lustrous hair is brushed and shining, and his beard shimmers in the morning light. God, I want his face in my pussy. I'm close, so close.

If he can still hear my desires he doesn't react, but he seems to know that I don't want him to go. "I made breakfast the human way," he smiles. "No magic. It took a while."

"Th...ah...thank you."

"Are you okay, Holly? You seem a little distracted."

The petulant device switches to a flurry of frenzied licks and sucks, and I can't... I can't hold it off any longer. My eyes screw tight, and my lips part as I gasp. I come, gripping the bed sheets at my sides.

Claus groans, a deep and longing sound which sets off the flutters in my lower belly, and before I know it, he's sat on the edge of the bed, opening the tie on his robe and gripping his cock in his hand. "Holly…"

My legs shake as I stand, the thing still licking me, and I do what I'd been daydreaming about all through Christmas dinner yesterday. I straddle Santa's lap, and I get exactly what I want for Christmas. I ride him, face-to face, his thick, magical cock filling me perfectly, not so big it hurts after last night, but just right and curved enough to reach my G-spot. He's perfect for me, hitting all the right places, and all I can do is groan his name.

"Holly," he whispers again, tangling his fingers in my hair. "Tell me what you want."

"You." It's all I can think of, all that matters in the world. I come again, my pussy clenching around his cock. God, every time I fuck him it feels like I might die from the pleasure. "I want to keep… keep doing this. Oh, fuck."

I trail my hands over his chest, raking my nails over his taut nipples. He pulls me into his kiss, deep and hungry and savage, and all I can do is keep coming, keep riding that rock-hard curvy candy cane.

I cry out in protest as he pulls out of me, but in the blink of an eye he has me turned around and bent over in front of him. My ass is right in his face as he licks my wet pussy, and pumps his cock in his fist. It feels good, so good, two tongues fucking me, a robotic one on my clit, one in my pussy. Hot cum splashes my legs as his muffled moans vibrate against my cunt. His tongue slips into me again and again and he has to hold me up as I come once more, my legs buckling beneath me. I can't go on like this. Any moment I'll pass out from the pleasure.

"I...can't turn...it... off." I sob as my next orgasm builds. I don't want it to end. Not ever.

He says nothing, just sits there behind me, catching his breath and kissing my pussy as it quivers right in front of him. I grip the edge of my dresser, watching myself in the mirror, the way my heavy tits hang and sway as I struggle to stay on my feet. The reflection of him watches me, hunger setting his gaze alight.

"Claus?"

"You've had enough?"

I nod, my face blazing scarlet as I come again, and this time I squirt, hot fluid flooding down my thighs. Claus's soft, warm lips kiss my lower back before he does as I ask. At the touch of his hand, the device falls away from my oversensitive clit. I'm free. I'm barely conscious, but I'm free.

I breathe into the crook of my elbow until I can finally think straight. "Thank you."

A wicked grin spreads across his face. "Good morning."

"Morning," I mutter as I burn with shame. Caught with my hands trapped in the cookie jar, or rather my clit trapped in some diabolical orgasm machine direct from Santa's workshop. Po-tay-toe, po-tah-toe.

He stands, tying up his robe, but leaving a deep V of chest exposed. "Holly?"

It takes all my effort to meet his eyes, but when I do, I'm glad. There's nothing but adoration there.

A small chuckle shakes his chest. "You're so beautiful."

"So are you," I tell him. "And I'm famished."

My embarrassment is gone and all I care about now is him and the scent of golden buttered toast and fresh coffee. I lift the tray from the dresser, and move to climb onto the bed.

"Um." He grimaces a little as I turn to face him. "You should probably clean up before you get on the bed. I'm sorry."

"Oh…" I chuckle, glancing down to my feet, where his cum gleams on my skin. Literally. It's pearlescent, like thick white shimmering bubble bath, and it smells faintly of peppermint. Which reminds me, I need to head to Bubble Bath and Body World and see what they have on clearance after the holidays.

He walks toward me, concern furrowing the gap between his bushy brows. "I'm sorry for the mess. I just… I don't know what would happen if I did it inside you."

"We need to be more careful," I agree. "I'm definitely not ready for any Santa babies."

"Well, we're different species, so I don't even know if that could happen. But I also don't know how your body would react to having my cum inside you. I don't want you to get sick."

Ah, yeah that would be kind of hard to discuss with my gyno. Besides, I actually don't mind the jizz on my legs. At the time it felt right, and the peppermint scent really helps freshen my room. "Agreed."

"I'll keep breakfast warm," he says gently and reassuringly. "Why don't you take a bath?"

"I'd love to, but I don't have a bath. I'll just hop in the shower." I'm more than a little salty about that fact. My house's previous owners delighted in telling me they had the antique clawfoot tub ripped out of the upstairs bathroom, and a new power shower installed. Suddenly all my fantasies of soaking in the luxurious tub were washed down the drain, along with my products.

"Pity," he says as he takes the tray from me and sets it on the bed. Gently, he takes my hand. His lips press soft and warm against my knuckles and there's a glimmer of mischief in those sapphire eyes. "I know how much you wanted one."

"Wait..." I narrow my eyes suspiciously as I edge toward the ensuite bathroom door. Ribbons and sex toys are one thing, but he can't have seriously upgraded my bathroom.

He glances up at the corner of the ceiling, his eyes wide and innocent as he fights off a smile.

"Claus, you didn't. You can't have."

"I don't know what you mean."

He has.

I squeal as I open the bathroom door, and find the most beautiful, enormous white bathtub filled with steaming water. It's perfect, from the red rose petals floating on the water's surface, to the ornate gold feet.

"Oh Claus, you did all this?" I beam, throwing my hair into a messy bun. A longing to sink into that steaming rose-scented water pulls me into the bathroom. Embarrassingly, I'm a little teary eyed over the gesture. "Did you have to rearrange all the plumbing for this?"

He nods. "You like it?"

"I love it! Thank you. It's wonderful."

"It's all for you." He kisses the back of my neck, sending a tingle through my body, as if I haven't come enough already today. "Merry Christmas, Holly."

"You didn't have to do this. Thank you."

He chuckles, tilting my chin toward him with his fingertips. He kisses me gently, lovingly, turning my knees to jelly. "I like to give."

I almost swoon as he tucks a stray strand of my hair behind my ear and bites his lip, stepping back to let me get into the tub.

CHAPTER FIVE

When I was little, Claus didn't come to my home on Christmas Eve.

Other kids in my class returned after the holidays, brimming with excitement, showing off the new toys Santa had brought them for being so good. I was met with awkward glances and whispers in the hallways.

After the incident, I didn't ask Santa for toys or games or anything like that. I only wanted one thing; for the terrible, awful thing I'd done to be reversed.

I wanted it undone with my whole heart, with every tear which rolled down my cheek and soaked into my pillow. I wrote to him that first year, after mom and I temporarily moved in with Aunt Ivy. I sent Santa letter after letter, wish after wish, burning them all in the fireplace so he would magically hear my plea. I did extra chores to rack up good points. I used my manners, I rescued a turtle from the road, I put my pocket money in collection boxes, and cuddled my mom when she sobbed and sobbed. I was a goddamn paragon of a child.

But not good enough.

I was evil. I'd done something really terrible, something I would never be forgiven for. It was easier just to hate Christmas and suffer the ache of jealousy, rejection, and grief I felt every December twenty-fifth. It was easier to deny his whole existence.

But now, sitting in this bath of steaming water, surrounded by velvety scarlet petals, I don't feel bad at all. As a matter of fact, I feel very good indeed. And I definitely don't want to know if my childhood suspicions were grounded in the truth.

Am I beyond redemption? That's a question I can never ask him, so I tuck it away, in the darkened corners of my heart.

Cleaning myself with a creamy bar of soap, I glance at the door connecting to my bedroom. He's out there, as real as I am. Santa Claus is out there waiting for me. I'm still pretty tired after our sessions last night and this morning, so I secretly hope he isn't expecting more sex when I get out of the tub. I want to get to know him better, I want to understand him.

My heart flutters just thinking about him. I need to stop that. It's dangerous. Giving your heart to someone always comes with risks, but when that someone is immortal and you're not... well... how can it have a happy ending? Especially not for him.

I know first-hand what it's like to watch someone you love die.

No. No, I'm not thinking about that. Pushing those thoughts away with the others, I sink down into the water, letting it cover my head completely. My steady pulse beats loud in my ears as I hold my breath. Soap bubbles crackle as they break the water's surface above me.

This is the dream; a bathtub I can fully submerge myself in, but I miss Claus, I realize. It makes me feel more than a little pathetic, but even though he's only in the next room I wish he was here with me.

When I come up for air, there's a gentle knock at the door.

I don't speak, not out loud anyway. In my mind I think about how much I wish he was here, sitting behind me, helping wash my hair.

The first touch of his hands doesn't startle me, because I sort of know it's coming. His strong fingers lather shampoo in my hair, working in tight circles all around my head. At once I'm at ease, sighing and leaning back against the edge of the tub.

How can this be? How can a man I barely know make me feel so whole?

"I have a question," I say, my voice sounding dreamy and faraway to my ears.

"Hm?"

"You can change sizes. I've seen you grow bigger, and I've seen you disappear up through my stove."

"Yes…"

"What is your…like, your default size?"

He chuckles as he pours a steady stream of warm water over my hair, rinsing away the suds. "I don't have one. I'm whatever size I choose to be. Whatever size fits best."

I twist around to face him. He looks like a bigger than average human guy, just as he has all morning. "But whenever I see you, you're usually like this."

"Because this is most comfortable for you. Last night, I grew for you because I thought you'd like it. On Christmas Eve I can shrink to get into people's homes, and grow to make carrying the heavy gifts easier."

"How does that work?"

He shrugs. "I don't know.

I laugh. "How can you not know?"

"Do you know how every function of your body works?"

"No, but there are scientists who do."

"But there's no one else like me," he says patiently. "I can't know everything by myself. I'm just a toymaker, not a scientist."

"I suppose." I sigh, though my curiosity is far from satisfied, and turn away from him, resuming my bath. "Well how big are you at home?"

He pauses, and a deep contemplative hum rolls through his chest. "I never paid attention. I'm just however big I need to be."

Now it's my turn to hum thoughtfully. It's a nifty trick, one of many he has at his disposal. I try to picture him at his workshop, a vast warmly lit space filled with wonderful things. He must take such meticulous care over everything he makes, and since there are no elves, he does it all himself. All that love comes from him alone.

It's endearing to think about, but practically, it means him working with superhuman speed, non-stop to fulfil the desires of a rapidly growing population. If I were to go back there with him, he wouldn't be around to stuff my goose as often as I'd like. Which, judging by how I've been constantly turned on since we met, would probably be all the time.

He nuzzles my cheek, wrapping his arms around me. "You're pondering."

"You're a lot to ponder," I tell him, leaning into his touch.

"Would it help if I shrunk?"

I chuckle. "No, I like you at this size."

A fluffy white robe appears at the side of the tub, ready for when I get out. Like everything else he's given me, it's sumptuous and perfect. Far more than I deserve.

"Holly?" He cups his hands at the top of my shoulders, his touch gliding across my wet skin. Every time he touches me, I feel my blood start to burn in the most delicious way. "What do you want to do today?"

I was so caught up in now I'd forgotten there was a whole day ahead of us. I hadn't even had breakfast yet. "What are my options?"

He smooths his hands over my shoulders, massaging my muscles, erasing the ache of being bound and fucked into oblivion last night. "Well, do you want me to stay?"

My heart leaps to my throat as I twist around to look at him once more. "Of course. You can read my desires, can't you? You know I want you to stay."

"I can hear your desires, yes. But I can't hear your reservations, your doubts. And I may not be human and I may live thousands of miles away from humans, but I know that often desire and doubt tangle. Wants can be complicated."

He stands and wipes his wet hands on a fluffy white towel. As he steps around to face me, I can't help but notice the sleeves of his robe are rolled up to reveal his thick, muscle-corded forearms. I silently tell my sex drive to chill the fuck out for a second.

Claus arches an eyebrow. "My forearms? Really?"

I shrug and flash him an innocent smile. "You're hot."

"So are you. And if it was just up to me, I'd want to see you every day. But it isn't just up to me. This feels good. Being with you feels good, but if you want me to leave, know that I'll go whenever you want me to. You need your boundaries, I know that—"

"Claus?"

His big chest heaves. "Holly?"

"I want you to stay."

If there were tiny chips of ice in my heart, his relieved smile melts them. "Thank you," he beams, as though I've just given him the greatest gift in the world.

Okay, I do have my doubts, and since he admitted he can't hear them, I don't feel so bad about thinking about them. He's Santa Claus for fuck's sake, and I'm pretty sure he saw my asshole this morning. But he's so good to me, and the sex is… supernatural. I'm not about to throw all that away because our affair could ruin childhoods. It's not like I had much of one to ruin anyway.

I stand and step into the robe as he holds it open for me. I've never felt anything so soft and fluffy in all my life. And it has pockets. I am so living in it forever. Turning around to face him, I can't help but grin. This is... it's everything I've ever wanted from a relationship; the comfort, the passion, the intimacy, the orgasms. It just never occurred to me that I'd be getting it all from Claus.

"What do you get from this?" I ask, reaching up to touch one of the pure white curls beneath his ear. It's silk between my fingertips. "You've done so much for me, but what do you want in return?"

There's a touch of sadness in his smile. "I just like giving. I like to make you happy."

He leans in and kisses me, soft and slow and deep. A lover's kiss. It feels too good to be true, but he's here, he's real. Bad people aren't supposed to get nice things from Santa Claus, but perhaps, after all these years, I've finally been forgiven.

CHAPTER SIX

"Okay, so I know what I want to do today," I say between mouthfuls of warm buttered toast. I'm unashamed to admit I'm on my fourth slice. Whatever Claus has done to this stuff is life changing. The fluffy bread melts in my mouth, and the golden butter is just the right amount of salty. If I had nothing but this toast to eat for the rest of my life, I'd be just fine with it.

He's reclining on his side beside me, leaning on his elbow and resting his head on the palm of his hand. The deep V at the neckline of his red robe is giving me a marvelous eyeful of silver chest hair. "Oh? You do?"

I nod, swallowing. I'm tempted to grab a fifth slice, but I'm pretty stuffed. Besides, I'd like to get moving. I want to see his sleigh.

His expression shifts, only slightly, but enough that I wonder if I've committed a Santa faux pas. The gentle warmth in his eyes, cools, and leaves behind a cagey cold. "My sleigh?"

"If that's okay?"

I wait, holding my breath as he sits in silence, contemplating my request. Finally, he turns his head to face me. "I don't know if you can. No-one human has ever seen it."

This is clearly a big deal for him so I don't push it. I just take one of the coffee mugs and take a sip. As good as he is at making toast, he makes a pretty crappy coffee. But he tried, and I'm so parched I'll drink anything. But jeez, what I wouldn't give for a decent cup of coffee. Still, I swallow the weak drink and offer him a reassuring smile.

"Oh no," he sits up. "I did it wrong, didn't I?"

"No, not at all. It's delicious."

"You just wished you had a decent cup of coffee though."

Fuck. Okay so sometimes his Santa powers won't work in my favor. "I promise it's wonderful."

I need to find some way to shut down the critical part of my brain. He'd made the coffee himself, the non-magical way. He made it with care just for me. I think very loudly that I wish he would know how hot he looks right now, flashing his chest as me.

A wide smile plumps his cheeks. "You flirt."

I grin and continue sipping and it's the most deliciously smooth coffee I've ever had in my life, deep, rich, exactly how I like it…that sneaky—

"Would you mind if I showered?" He asks as if he hasn't just meddled with my breakfast.

I sigh, setting the coffee down. "Not at all."

I get up to show him how to work it and where the towels are. He follows me into the bathroom, and I realize as I'm explaining it all to him that he can probably just use his magic for this stuff. Still, he listens intently, nodding his head as I explain how finicky the shower control can be. "Just yell if you need anything."

"Thank you." He smiles and begins to untie his robe.

Despite the fact I've already bathed I desperately want to get into the shower with him. The thought of having his body wet and slippery against mine is such a turn on, but I need to get dressed and figure out what else we could do today since seeing his sleigh is apparently not an option.

So, I step out and give him some privacy and head back to the bedroom. It looks pretty cold out, so I pull out a pair of jeans and a thick green sweater. Maybe we could take a walk and he could bang me up against a tree, or maybe we could go out for lunch and he could bang me in a restroom, or maybe...

God, I need to chill.

The sound of sloshing water teases me. I can't help but picture him, naked and wet, the soap bubbles running over the curves of his big broad torso. Flutters roll down through my belly, growing even more intense as his gasps and groans emerge above the sound of the water.

Quickly, before I get that damned contraption stuck on my clit again, I head out of the bedroom and make my way downstairs to wash the breakfast dishes. I'm almost at the bottom when I freeze. My floor is different. There used to be fake (but pretty convincing at first glance) wooden floors, but now it's unmistakably hardwood, the kind I've always wished I had. My tattered hallway rug is now thick and luxurious, the baseboard is no longer chipped behind the door. Once I start looking for them, the changes are obvious and numerous.

Making my way through to the kitchen, I notice more things he's tampered with. A new dishwasher, a big fridge with an ice machine, a fresh coat of paint, gleaming marble kitchen tiles. It's all stuff I've wanted forever, things I've dreamed about while watching home improvement shows. It's perfect. So why doesn't it feel perfect?

Am I being ungrateful? Probably.

Most people would be appreciative of mind-blowing sex with someone who can grant your every desire, but it might have been nice to be asked. Because if he had asked, this isn't what I would have wanted. Not really.

I take a deep breath and push it out. I'm being a brat. Claus has done so many wonderful things for me, and we haven't even been together for a full day. I rinse the dishes and put them in my new fancy dishwasher and head to the living room, trying to appreciate the excitement of the brand-new TV beside the enormous stone fireplace where my little woodburning stove used to be. Two plush cream overstuffed sofas sit facing each other on opposite sides of the hearth. And, oh, hey, my Christmas tree is fuller, better lit, fancier ornaments...

This is nice.

It's nice.

Lovely. Honestly.

I'm totally not freaking out.

The few Christmas cards I got are neatly arranged on the mantle above the cozy fire. They're decorated with snowmen, little bunnies sat in the snow, bright red cardinals eating holly berries, and him. I smile as I pick up the card my grandma sent. My dad's mom. She rarely talks to me, and honestly, I can't blame her. Her only grandchild who took everything from her. But she sends me cards at Christmas.

The Santa Claus on the card isn't nearly as sexy as the real life one. He's an adorable cartoon character and he isn't alone. Kissing his cheek, is an equally adorable and jolly lady in a bright red dress and a snow-white apron.

Shit. How did I forget to ask him about Mrs. Claus?

Wildfire spreads beneath the surface of my skin, a mixture of shame and embarrassment. Am I having an affair with a married man?

Those four slices of toast were a bad idea. I have to fight not to throw up as I try to come to terms with potentially the second worst thing I've ever done. Sinking down onto one of the new couches, I bury my head in my hands. I'm in way over my head, and I just wish I had someone to help me figure out what to do.

"Holly," he says softly, appearing right in front of me and soothing me with the sound of his voice. Silver snowflakes dust the floor between us. "Holly, what's wrong?"

I can't look at him. I can't look into those sapphire eyes, because I know I'll just want to fall into his arms. Shaking my head, I keep my lips shut tight. His warm hands cup my shoulders, gently caressing the tops of my arms as I fight back tears.

"If it's about the new furniture I can change it all back to how it was," he says. "I thought you'd like it."

"I do," I whisper. "It's all perfect, but I wish you'd asked me first."

"You're right. I wanted it to be a surprise. I saw how happy you were with the bath and I wanted to make you even happier, but I took it too far. I'm sorry. In the future, I'll ask."

I raise my eyes just a little. He just has a towel wrapped low on his hips and the sight of him gives me tingles. I want so badly to just hold him, but I want him to leave me alone too. I want to be alone to cry.

"Okay, I'll go."

"Stop it," I sniff. "That was private."

He shifts slightly, and I just know he's fighting off the urge to tell me he can't just turn off his abilities. But he doesn't say it. Instead, he gets up and sits on the couch opposite. The fire pops and crackles, comforting and soothing, filling the silence between us which has suddenly grown unbearable.

I'm so afraid. I'm afraid to ask him if he has a wife, because I'm terrified of the answer. Not only will I feel awful about myself, but I'll lose him.

I tear my eyes from the floorboards and allow myself to look at him. He's sweet and kind, huge, strong and white-haired, like a big magical polar bear. And right now, his otherworldly blue eyes are filled with human sadness and worry. I'm causing that.

I bite my lip and breathe deeply, gripping my own hand. I just need to be brave, swallow my fears and open up.

"I need to ask something, and I need you to be completely honest," I say. "You have to tell me the truth, okay?"

He nods. "Okay."

"Please don't lie to me."

"I would never."

"Okay." The room spins around me a little. This could be the end. "I should have asked this right at the start, before this began. Is there a Mrs. Claus?"

His lips close, and that same far-off iciness hardens his face. Okay, so I guess that's my answer. I should have remembered that if something seems too good to be true, it's because it is.

"Oh God." I stand so sharply I grow lightheaded. "Is there?"

"Holly..."

"Is there?"

He looks down at himself, unable to meet my eyes. I'm shaking, my jaw clenched so tight it feels as though my teeth will shatter.

"There was," he says, his deep voice barely a whisper. "But not anymore. She's... gone."

He lifts his head, those blue eyes shining with tears, and I realize the horrible truth I've known all my life. I really am an awful person.

"Claus, I'm so sorry."

"You didn't know. I should have told you right away but everything felt so perfect. I didn't want to bring it up."

I shake my head and step toward him, climbing onto his lap and straddling his thighs. His arms almost crush me, squeezing the air from my lungs, but I'll happily stay here as long as he needs me. When I'm in his arms I can't even fathom why I was annoyed at him for redecorating and upgrading my little house. I can't think of anything other than that I want him to feel better.

Of course, he hears that desire. Slowly he lifts his head and smiles. "Thank you. But I'm okay. I've had over a century to come to terms with the loss. I just don't want to push you away."

"Neither do I."

I kiss him, wrapping my arms around his neck and sinking into the softness and warmth of him. My fingers skate across his chest and drift down to his round stomach. The fluffy towel at his hips could so easily fall away, and even though I'm tired and a little raw I find myself desperately wanting him again.

He growls in approval against my lips, and his kiss grows deeper, his hands drifting down my back toward the curve of my ass.

"Again?" He whispers as he slips a hand beneath the waistband of my jeans, gripping my ass cheek with his big, strong fingers.

"I want to. God I really do, but I need a rest, just for a little while." I'm just not used to this much sex in such a short span of time.

"That's okay," he smiles, kissing my lips gently, bringing his hand out of my jeans and stroking feathery circles at the small of my back. His touch sends sparks through my veins. I'm still horny, and even if I'm not going to fuck him, I still want to do something. I want to make him feel good.

I look down at him, at the firm swell of his cock bulging against the towel between my thighs. And I know what I want.

His breath hitches as his Santa powers detect my desires and the scenario plays out in his mind. The rhythm of his chest becomes sharp and shallow as his excitement grows. Whenever he comes his jizz smells like peppermint, and now, I want to lick that candy cane.

"Are you sure?" He asks, his deep voice hoarse as I climb down from his lap.

I'm already on my knees, untucking the end of his towel from his hip. "I want to taste you."

He groans as he leans back against the cushions, thick thighs parted, his rigid cock standing to attention and straining toward me. I run my fingers through his silver pubes and up over the swell of his stomach, biting my lip as he flinches at my touch.

"Ticklish?"

He nods, his eyes half-closed as a bead of clear pre-cum slides down the underside of his shaft. He definitely doesn't seem to mind, so I run my fingertips down his sides, making him squirm, working my way lower until I can run my nails along the lengths of his thighs. A gasp escapes him as he wriggles, and his cock bounces just an inch from my lips.

Leaning forward, I take him into my mouth, cupping his balls in my hands as I suck his dick. He moans, deep and low, his hips bucking against the couch as I lick the length of him.

"Holly…" He whispers as I take him deeper.

My lips and tongue slide up and down, each stroke earning me a desperate, deep, and breathless moan. He's the perfect size, not so long I have to fight and gag to take him all, but thick and hot against my tongue.

And mine.

Right now, he's all mine. At this moment, I'm the only thing that matters to him in the whole world. Christmas could come and go, and he'd still be here, his head back against the couch cushions, his throat bobbing, his knuckles pale as he grips his thighs. I taste peppermint, fresh and sweet, and I know he's close. But I'm far from done with him.

I let my lips linger around the head of his cock as I pull back, and lick a long, slow stroke back down to the base of him. He groans. His fingers flex, desperate to finish himself off quickly.

I want this to last, I want him to feel so much pleasure he forgets everything except my name and the sensation of my mouth on his cock. So, I take his hands, lace our fingers together, and pin them to the seat of the couch.

His breath is heavy and irregular as I lick him, fluttering my tongue against the head of his cock, before sucking it between my lips. I love how his eyes crease as he squeezes them shut, how his toes curl either side of my knees.

He's powerless as I pleasure him. This big man is completely at my mercy and clearly loving every second of it. The broken, yearning sounds coming from him are like nothing I've ever heard.

"Does this feel good?" I ask, before licking the side of his cock from base to tip, keeping my eyes on his.

"So good," he groans. His blushing chest rises sharply and his belly tightens. He's barely holding on, and the scarlet flush of his cheeks is just about the sexiest thing I've ever seen. I suspect that if I took all of him into my mouth, he'd be finished in just a few bobs of my head. But I love teasing him.

I shift lower and lick his balls, grinning to myself as his eyes widen and he grinds his hips against the couch. His fingers tighten in mine and his thighs tremble at either side of me. I want to do this all day. Hell, I want to do it for the rest of my life.

He nods eagerly, closing his eyes once more. I guess he's okay with that idea. So, I take my time, exploring every inch of him, savoring the taste of him. Releasing my grip on his hands, I stroke his shaft and cup his balls.

"Please," he whispers, twisting his fists into the couch cushions.

"You want to come?"

"Yes. Faster. Please."

His cheeks are so pink, and that same shade flushes across his chest and belly. I raise up to lick his nipples, still slowly sliding my hands up and down his cock. He moans and my pussy aches with need for him, but this is all for him. He can pay me back later.

His nipple stiffens beneath my tongue and I can tell he likes the attention there, but what he really needs right now is my mouth on his dick, hard and fast. I've had enough teasing too. I drop back down and take him all in my mouth, stroking him with my lips, following the engorged veins with my tongue. And I watch him. I watch him turn from pink to scarlet, the rise and fall of his chest and belly. He raises his arms, gripping the back of the couch as though he has to hold on for his life.

He cries out, "Oh…. Oh… OH!" and my mouth floods with the taste of sticky sweet peppermint. "Ffffuck."

When his breath returns to normal, I climb back up into his lap. I love that he's naked while I'm clothed, that his body still trembles with the aftershocks of the orgasm I gave him. He's over a thousand years old, and I know I just made him forget every moment in his life but this one. I feel powerful.

He keeps his eyes closed as he pulls me close and holds me. His heartbeats pound against my ear, hard and fast but growing slower by the minute. I find myself wondering if he is immortal or just has a very long lifespan. Will his big generous heart stop one day in the future? I don't know why I feel sad at that thought. Presumably by then I'll be long gone. Despite his white hair, he's not old by human standards. He doesn't seem like he has any plans on going in the next millennia or so.

Perhaps it's the thought of such an ancient and loving soul leaving this earth where there are no others like him. Perhaps it's the thought of children waking up one Christmas morning and finding he hasn't come to them that year. Or perhaps, it's because I'm in serious danger of falling for him. Whatever it is, my chest tightens, and a lump forms in my throat.

"Thank you," he whispers, smoothing his hand down my hair. "That was… incredible."

I sit back and flash him a smile. "I loved it, every second of it."

"I'm glad."

"And my breath is minty fresh, so that's pretty nifty."

His eyes crease as he chuckles. "Human men don't taste like me?"

I shake my head and bring up a hand to touch his blushing cheek. He's so handsome. I never thought I'd be lust-drunk over Santa Claus, but here I am, completely smitten. As he closes his eyes and leans into my touch, I kind of want to suck his dick all over again.

A brisk knock at the door puts an end to those thoughts. I clamber to my feet, fully aware that my curtains are open. There's a fair bit of distance between my neighbors and I so I never have to worry much about privacy, but then again, I've never had Santa bare-assed on my couch either.

He wraps his towel back around his waist and stands, eyes wide as though we've been caught doing something we shouldn't. As if we aren't two consenting single adults with the healthy urge to fuck each other constantly.

"Are you expecting someone?" He asks.

"No."

I head to the door, straightening my sweater and hoping my hair isn't too messy. It could just be a delivery guy, or a neighbor telling me their dog got out. But my heart is racing, and anxious and sweat prickles against my back. I turn around to check he's covered up, but Claus is nowhere to be seen. He definitely didn't run upstairs. Perhaps he's invisible? Can he do that? I make a mental note to ask him about all his superpowers and turn the latch on the door.

The sight which greets me sends that prickling sweat into a full-blown river. My mom stands on my doorstep tall and willowy, her hair dyed vibrant crimson. She rakes her gaze over me as I open the door fully, and her lips tighten in disapproval.

"Holly," she sighs. "I do wish you'd make an effort when you come to the door. I could've been the man of your dreams."

I force a smile and step back, giving her space to pass. "Come in, mom."

CHAPTER SEVEN

My mom is clearly confused as she walks through my new and improved house. Her head is on a swivel, and her eyes keep darting back to me, waiting for me to explain the sudden upgrades. I just smile, feigning innocence. What can I say? *I've been fucking Santa for the past twelve or so hours and he fixed up my house. You should call by in the spring when the easter bunny landscapes my whole back yard after I let him rim me.*

"It's festive in here," she says, narrowing her eyes.

"Oh, yes. Thank you."

"It's suspicious."

Ever since... ever since I was a child there's been a distance between us. I don't want to say she outright blames me, but...

She struggled. We both did.

She sits on the edge of the couch and glances at the paltry selection of cards on the mantle, then at the sprigs of mistletoe on the chandelier above as if they're going to pounce on her. "You left in such a hurry yesterday, your aunt Ivy said I should check in on you. She knows this time of year is difficult."

"I'm fine." I say instinctively. Usually it's a lie, but today I actually mean it. My heart is buzzing inside my chest, brimming with the excitement of this new and wonderful thing. With Claus, I feel like I'm glowing.

"That's good," she nods.

I recognize the sadness in her eyes. It's as familiar to me as her smile and her voice. "Are you okay?"

She shrugs. "The holidays are hard."

Fresh guilt claws at me. Usually, it's just the constant heaviness of what I've done to this family, but this new regret is staggering. And I know it's because I feel good. I shouldn't. I shouldn't be happy. I shouldn't be comfortable by a log fire in the arms of a man I just can't get enough of. None of it is deserved.

I should be mourning.

But I'm not. I'm happy, I'm swimming in warmth and affection from a guy I can hardly believe is real. And I want to be with him right this instant.

"Holly?" His deep voice startles me as he makes his way down the stairs. He's immaculate, dressed in a thick creamy fisherman style sweater and perfectly tailored jeans which accentuate his big thighs and peachy round butt. His hair is brushed back from his forehead, the ends curling just above his shoulders, and his beard and moustache are perfectly groomed.

My heart flutters at the sight of him, then almost stops as my mom stands up from the couch, her lips parted in shock.

"Oh...oh my," she stammers turning away from me. "I didn't realize you had company."

This can't be happening. It's obvious by the slow confidence with which he approaches that he's comfortable here in the house. As if that wasn't enough to raise my mom's suspicions, he walks over to me and puts one arm around my shoulder, holding me against him. The scent of soot floods the room, and my eyes widen as I realize he must have hidden in the chimney.

He holds a hand out toward my mom and flashes her a charming smile. "I'm Claus."

"Gabrielle," she replies, wide-eyed as she takes in the enormous white-haired man draped over her only daughter. "And you're…?"

He smiles again. "Claus."

"No, I mean… are you a friend of Holly's or…?"

I can't let him answer that. If this morning has revealed anything to me, it's that he isn't completely up to speed on human boundaries and societal expectations. "Yes, he's a friend of mine. Visiting for the holidays. He's from… Finland?"

"I came here for Christmas," he nods. "And I rearranged her plumbing."

I'll kill him.

My mom's eyes take a journey down the length of his big body, the cogs turning behind her eyes. She knows, I think. Some part of her knows he's Santa Claus, just as I knew right away, even though I didn't believe in him at all. And I'm absolutely certain she knows he isn't just a friend.

By the time her eyes return to his, she looks a little queasy. "Well, I just hope you're being careful."

"I am." He's beaming, so goddam pleased with himself and — I think — completely unaware of what he's implying. "I was very attentive. Holly was very, very satisfied."

My mom's mouth snaps shut as she blinks a few times, as if manually wiping the mental image from her brain. I cling to the hope that perhaps it doesn't sound as bad to her as it does to me, but then she shrugs and gives me a sly smile. "Well, I'm just glad you're having a good Christmas, for once."

Claus' grip falters at her words and I give my mom a 'stop talking' look. He doesn't know how much I hate Christmas, and he definitely doesn't know my reason for that, and right now I don't want him to. Yes, we have shared a lot since yesterday evening. Yes, I like him. But I don't feel ready at all to share my deepest and darkest secrets. Not yet. Not until I'm sure he won't hate me.

"I am," I smile, hiding my worries.

My mom looks over Claus once more. "I usually have to come round and put up her tree because Holly doesn't bother much with Christmas."

He stiffens, letting go of me so he can turn to face me. My cheeks blaze and my vision is shaking as I try to avoid both of them. I don't want to do this. Not now. Maybe not ever.

"Alright," I sigh. "Claus and I have a lot to do today. I'm showing him the local sights. Is it okay if I call you tomorrow, mom?"

The smile slips from her face. "Oh, yes. Not a problem."

I feel a little pang of guilt as I follow her through the living room and out toward the front door. I know this time of year is just as hard for her as it is for me, and perhaps seeing her daughter happy for once eases her own pain. But I have to protect my own heart too.

I step outside with her and hug her, breathing in the familiar scent of her. The air is cold and damp, and our breaths emerge as clouds. Squirrels scamper around the skeletal trees which surround my cozy house. In all the warmth and loveliness with Claus, I'd almost forgotten there was a world out here.

"Did I say something wrong?" She asks.

"No." I break the hug and offer her a weak, reassuring smile. "It's just very, very early days with Claus, and I haven't... I haven't told him about that Christmas."

"Ah." She nods. I can almost see a new fissure crack her heart. Her eyes become unbearably sad. "I understand how hard it must be for you to tell people about it, but please know it wasn't your fault."

"It was, I know—"

"You were a child, Holly." The sharpness in her tone silences me. "You know that none of us blame you."

But they do. I know they do. Whenever they've had too much to drink, they let slip about what I cost them. Just hints, but I know what they're saying. Whenever my mom or my dad's sister, Ivy, think I'm out of earshot they whisper, and exchange side-eyed glances at each other. They blame me, and I one hundred percent agree with their judgement.

I smile gratefully and wrap my arms around my chest, hugging myself hard. "Thank you for coming round."

"I just wanted to make sure you're okay. The house looks beautiful, by the way."

Glancing over my shoulder to the front door (which has recently been magically painted a bright festive red and decorated with a holly wreath) I can't help but smile—genuinely this time. "Claus has done a great job with the house. It's everything I've ever wanted."

"I'm really glad you're happy." She chuckles and narrows her eyes. "But don't you think he looks... I mean... sort of uncannily like..."

I fight back a laugh and feign ignorance. "Like what?"

Her eyebrows crease as she presses her lips together. I can tell there's a war raging between her manners and the obvious truth; he looks like Santa Claus. At last, she settles on, "He just looks like a nice man. Kind. Have fun, Holly. But please be careful."

"I will."

She gives me a last warm smile. "You smell very fresh and minty."

I die a little inside as I watch her walk to her car. Waving her off, relief lifts my spirits as she pulls away. I adore my mom, but right now I need time to figure out what these feelings mean. I like him. I really, really do. But this intensity is scary. I shouldn't be craving to be near him after such a short span of time. If he was any other man, I'd be playing it cool, but with him, I'm completely smitten and irrational.

Because he isn't just any other man. He's Santa Claus.

I've always been wary of age gaps in my relationships, but now I'm apparently dating a man over a thousand years old. I've spent most of my life hating Christmas and now all I can taste is peppermint. None of this makes sense, and if I'm honest, it scares me. But it excites me too. For now, I'm just going to enjoy it for what it is.

I turn around and head inside, sighing as the warm air of the house envelops me. Stepping into the cozy hallway, it feels like walking into another dimension filled with comfort and heat. I could get used to this.

As I head into the living room, Claus sits back on one of the couches, his arms spread wide across the backs of the cushions. He rocks forward and pulls himself to his feet as I approach, his grey brows crease in concern. "I messed up, didn't I?"

"Um...No, you're fine." I reply a little too hesitantly, causing his grey brows to crease together in worry. "It's just, usually we'd wait a couple of months before meeting parents."

"Ah."

"But I know you only came downstairs because I wanted you to. It's okay."

His cheeks round as he smiles and folds his arms across his big, broad chest. "Still, I'm sorry. I still have a lot to learn about human etiquette."

The way he says that gets my mind racing. Was Mrs. Claus human, or was she like him; supernatural, hundreds, if not thousands of years old? And if she was human, what era did she come from? Was she like me? Falling hard and fast for a man she barely understood with powers she can hardly comprehend, but absolutely loving the way he rails her.

I'm so curious about every aspect of him. Claus' life is like nothing I've ever known before, and now I'm a part of it, for better or for worse.

"So," he says. "Did you decide what you want to do today?"

"No," I shake my head and smile, stepping toward him so he envelops me in his arms. I'm safe and warm, and my world smells of gingerbread and woodsmoke.

He presses his lips to my forehead and breathes deeply, his chest heaving against me. God, he makes me feel so safe and warm and unbelievably horny. "I have an idea," he says. "But you have to promise to keep a secret."

CHAPTER EIGHT

It's cold, so cold my bones ache as I try to bundle myself as much as possible in my big winter coat. My boots are tight because I have two pairs of thick socks on, but we take the walk slowly, making our way through the bare trees. Claus walks beside me in his fisherman's sweater and jeans, completely comfortable in the freezing temperature.

"You're not cold?" I ask him through chattering teeth.

He chuckles and pulls me closer. His body is practically a furnace and moments later I'm thawed out. "This is warm compared to home."

My jaw clenches at the thought. "What's it like?"

"Hm?"

"Your home."

He pulls in a deep breath and sends a shimmering cloudy breath into the air. "Very quiet... cold."

"Do you get lonely?"

"Sometimes."

His answer forms a knot in my stomach. At some point he's going to have to go back there, and there's no way I can just drop everything and go there with him.

I clear my throat in the hopes I can dislodge some of the nervous flutters in my chest. "How often do you get to come here?"

"To your home? I've never been before."

"No," I stop walking and try to think how to phrase it. "To...the mortal world."

His lips quirk, confirming my suspicions that it was an overblown and dramatic thing to say. "Just at Christmas."

"Oh."

"It takes a long time to make all the gifts. There are over 2 billion children on earth, though of course, not all of them get presents."

Trying to ignore the sting his last comment left behind, I pin my arms firmly to my sides in an attempt to generate some warmth. "So, when do you have to go back?"

The question hits him hard. A shift in his eyes fills me with dread, and I know it's soon. I literally feel my heart sink.

God, what's wrong with me? I hardly know this guy and I'm dangerously attached. I can't be. This thing, whatever it is, can never work in the long term. I need to keep reminding myself it's a short and extremely sweet affair, nothing more.

Forcing a smile, I step toward him and link my arm with the crook of his elbow, immediately glad of the warmth. "I suppose we should make the most of the time we have."

He nods, and a quiet chuckle sounds in his throat. "I would like that."

We set off again, walking through the cold, wet woods. Our winter wonderland walk consists of bleak, grey skies, bare trees, and mushy dead leaves underfoot. "It's a shame it isn't snowing, so at least it would look pretty for you."

"Actually, I prefer this," he says as he helps me over a fallen tree. "White Christmases are beautiful to look at, yes, but snow makes the roads so perilous. With so many travelling to see their loved ones, so many cars filled with children…I'd rather people stay safe than suffer an accident. No one should be left grieving, especially not at Christmas."

He's too close to the truth, and it gets my back up. A fuck-up at Christmas is worth a hundred fuck-ups any other time of the year.

"Why?" I grumble, painfully aware of how callous I sound. "What makes Christmas so special?"

He glances toward me, hurt sharpening his features. "Because it's a time for generosity, for loved ones to come together and celebrate."

I bite my tongue. I'm not going to argue with him over this, especially not when our time together is so short. Still, I feel a lump forming in my throat, and I have to distract myself by peering through the trees so I don't tear up.

Claus stops walking and turns to face me. "Are you sad?"

"No," I lie. "Just cold."

He takes a step forward and holds out his arms, and without hesitation I fall into them. He has grown since we left my house, and now he's so big and husky I can't get my hands to meet at his back. He's soft and warm, and I don't want him to go. I don't want this to end. Why of all the people in the world did it have to be him?

He arches his back toward me, his shoulders slouching as he kisses the top of my head and his hands stroke my hair. "You can talk to me, you know." His deep voice rumbles in his chest by my ear. "Whatever it is that's hurting you..."

"It's nothi—" I stop myself before the lie can escape. "I'm sorry."

"It's okay. If you want to talk—"

"I just...can we forget the world for a little bit?"

"Of course." He places his hands at either side of my jaw and tilts my head toward him.

Sinking through the silken silver of his beard to find his lips, I feel the earth drop from beneath me. As long as I live, I know I'll never find another man who kisses me like Claus does. Nothing else matters right now. Just him, his lips, the gentle tug of his teeth on my lower lip. If he doesn't stop soon, I'm going to have to let him fuck me right here in the cold, wet mud.

The temperature plummets.

I pull back from his embrace and open my eyes, and the world has changed. Instead of trees we stand surrounded by a vast open plain. Frost sparkles on each blade of grass so that they look pale blue instead of green. The plain goes on for miles and miles in all directions. It's stunning, but I've no idea where we are. There's no sign of life anywhere, other than a group of distant brown shapes I think might be horses or cows.

"How did we get here?" I sweep back my hair as it blows in the gentle icy breeze. "Santa magic?"

He chuckles and nods. "Yes, Santa magic." Stepping behind me, he wraps his arms around me once more and kisses the back of my neck until I forget the cold. "Look up to the sky."

I lean back against him, basking in the sensation of having his big, warm body pressed against me like that. But then my eyes trail up and I just about fall back onto him. The sky is blue and bright, but the moon is enormous, hanging directly over us. And beside that, is another, smaller moon. Except the second one is surrounded by rings.

"Claus?" I'm terrified, my stomach is turning cartwheels, and my chest is tight. I'm by no means a space scientist, but it doesn't take a genius to figure out that this isn't earth.

"It's okay," he whispers, tightening his grip around me. "You're safe. Nothing can hurt you."

Hurt me? No, it's not hurt I'm afraid of. Frankly I'm more afraid that I've been zapped into space by a man I've only known for a day. I can't breathe. "What have you done, Claus?" I spin around to face him, my eyes scanning his face. "Where have you taken me?"

"To my home." His grip around me loosens as concern registers on his face. His lips part and his eyes grow wide. "I thought you wanted to see it."

"I did, but I thought it would be on earth."

A nervous smile breaks through his worry, like the distant winter sun shining through snow clouds. "Holly, your world is too small for me to hide in. Every corner of it is monitored. If I stayed there then people would know for certain that I'm real."

"Why is that a bad thing?"

He sighs. "Because I'm one man. I need children to stop believing in me at some point, otherwise I wouldn't have time to sleep, or even to breathe. I don't visit them when they're babies and too little to believe, and I stop visiting when they're too old to believe in magic."

I run my hands over the top of my head and raise my eyes to the sky once more. The enormous planets overhead look like something from a sci-fi novel. I wonder how far from home I am, and how much time it took for us to get here. I doubt we're even in the same solar system. A wave of nausea churns in the bottom of my stomach.

"Am I trapped here?" I ask, terrified of the answer. I don't have much going for me on earth, but at least it's familiar. It's home. My mom is there.

"No. My goodness, no, Holly." His eyes widen as he takes my hand and presses my freezing fingers to his warm lips. "As soon as you want to go home just say it and I'll take you. You have my word."

"Did we fly through space?"

"No and yes. It's... I think you say 'a pocket dimension'? I can travel between our worlds. I just held onto you and brought you with me."

My head is spinning with a million questions and fears. Despite his reassurance, I just want to cry. I pull my hand from his, ignoring the bitter cold. "This is a lot... You could have pre-warned me."

"I'm sorry. I wanted it to be a surprise. You said you wanted to forget the world and I thought this might help." His breaths come out uneven as he shakes his head. "I thought this is what you wanted."

"It is. I mean— I thought—" I have to look away from him, away from those sorrowful sapphire eyes. "When you take me back home, how much time will have passed?"

"Oh, none at all. The journey is instantaneous and time moves differently here. That's how I can make so many toys in the span of one of your years. I promise, everything is okay."

I breathe deeply and nod. That's a huge relief and I suppose it makes sense if I don't think about it too hard. "I trust you, it's just such a lot."

"I'm so sorry."

How can a man so big and strong look so utterly helpless? I know I'm a sucker, but as he looks at me with those damn puppy dog eyes, the fear and annoyance ebbs from me. When all's said and done, there are a lot of positive sides to my current situation.

I might well be the first human to step foot on this planet and witness all this beauty. I'm an explorer, a pioneer. And I'm here with the sexiest man I've ever met, AND he likes to make me come. All in all, I'm living the good life.

"What's this place called?" I ask him.

"I never gave it a name," he says. "I just call it home."

I'm not going to call it that, in case he gets the wrong idea and magically transports all my stuff here, so I dub it Planet Santa in my head. "It's very beautiful."

"Then it's worthy of you," he smiles. "How about from now on, even if I hear your desires, I don't act on them right away? I'll wait until you tell me."

I consider it for a moment. It's wonderful having my every desire fulfilled. It's also somehow just too much. "Yeah. I think that would help. Unless we're in bed. I like when you pay attention to my desires when we're in bed."

"Agreed. I will do that," he smiles. "Would you still like to see my workshop?"

"I'd love to."

With a smile he offers me his hand, and I'm only too happy to take it. When I'm this close to him even the cold can't reach me. Claus makes me feel safe and warm. He makes me feel appreciated and important.

"Would you like to walk, or is it okay if I use my magic?"

Happiness balloons inside me at his question. That he's asking for my input rather than just deciding for me means the world. I give his hand a little squeeze "How far is it?"

"From here..." He raises his eyes to the horizon and squints. "Maybe... six hundred miles."

"Oh." I guess it's the thought that counts. "Magic me, please."

Claus nods and turns to face me, wrapping his big, strong arms around me. I nestle close to him, loving the softness and warmth of his body against mine, and already wondering if it'll be possible for us to have at least a quickie here before he takes me back to my home.

An ear-splitting, blood-freezing roar cuts off my thoughts.

The earth shakes, a shadow blots out the sunlight, and a white bear the size of a two-story house snarls at us.

And wouldn't you know it, I left my broadsword at home.

CHAPTER NINE

The polar bear monster snarls.

Each one of its ferociously sharp, serrated teeth is longer than my forearm and twice as thick. I don't scream. I can't. Screaming requires breath, and right now that's out of the question.

All I can do is cling to Claus and hope the monster kills us quickly. My mom will be left mourning through another Christmas, only this time her grieving will be accompanied by the agony of never knowing what happened to me. Will she suspect Claus, I wonder? Will they put me on the news saying I was last seen with a man from Finland who looked suspiciously like Santa?

"Get behind me," Claus commands, his voice deep and steady.

But I don't move. I remain pressed against him, gripping the front of his sweater as if my hands are iron vices. The thought of watching him die is too much to handle. I'd rather die in his arms.

"Holly—"

"I'm not leaving you," I cry out.

He gives me no choice. Claus begins to grow, bigger and taller until I can no longer hold on to him.

And he keeps growing, far larger than I've ever seen him. I have to step back in case he accidentally crushes me beneath his foot. Within moments he's even taller than the bear. His enormous fingers curl into fists as he marches toward the beast with intimidating purpose, the ground shaking with his steps.

I can hardly stand to look as Claus approaches the monster. Yes, I'm terrified of it, but that doesn't mean I want it to suffer. I cover my eyes, unable to watch the man who until now has been nothing but gentle turn into some bear-wrestling titan.

Claus' voice echoes across the plain, deep and almost lyrical as he speaks in a language I don't understand. The bear roars back, so loud it almost throws me off balance and makes the world spin around me. And then Claus speaks again, firmly, but patiently.

As I peer through the cracks between my fingers, the bear's snout grows smooth, and its lips descend to cover its teeth. In just a few seconds it looks less like a monster and more like a big, kind of goofy-looking animal.

Claus continues to speak to the bear in his special Santa language and the creature shoots me a sideways glance. It almost seems as though it understands. And then, without a drop of blood shed, the once savage, snarling monster meekly backs away, and then trundles across the plain, sniffing the air and wagging its stubby tail.

"What…" I stand with my mouth agape. "How?"

"Santa magic," Claus says beside me, back to his regular big boy stature. "I just told him we didn't want to fight and we weren't at all tasty, and that I thought his fur was very majestic. Bears are quite vain."

"You can speak to animals?"

"Animals from here, yes. Also, dogs in your world. I have to tell them to be quiet when I enter the houses. And I'm currently learning goose. They can be quite astute guards."

I nod as I file away yet more impossible information. "Neat."

Claus' chest deflates as he pushes out a breath. Up to this point, he seemed cool, calm and collected but now I see his hands are trembling a little.

"Are you okay?" I ask.

He nods before opening his arms wide to embrace me. This time, I step onto my tiptoes and wrap my arms around his shoulders, pulling him down to me. He nuzzles my neck and sighs.

"Thank you," I say. "That was so brave."

"I just couldn't stand the thought of you getting hurt," he whispers as his hands caress the curve at the small of my back. His nuzzles turn to kisses, stealing my breath and making my heart skip as his hands drop lower to my butt.

Right away my body heats, thrumming with just one need, one desire: him. "Claus…" I whisper his name against his ear as my hands grasp the thick creamy wool of his knitted sweater. I want him out of it. I want my naked body against his, right here, right now.

"I want you too, but out here, we would be cold," he chuckles.

"Then warm me up."

"Do you still want me to take you to the workshop?"

"Yes."

His teeth nip at my shoulder as I tilt my head away from him, giving him access to my neck. A flurry of ice crystals whirl around us as he kisses me, his big, strong arms surrounding me.

I'm warm. Deliciously, comfortably warm. I open my eyes and find we're no longer out on the plain, but standing inside a cozy room. A fire crackles gently in a fireplace, casting copper light around us. The air smells like baking pastry and burning pine. My heart skips with the realization of where he brought us.

"Is this your home?"

He raises his head and smiles. "Yes."

I don't know what I expected. Perhaps an enormous warehouse with conveyor belts full of dolls and rocking horses. Or maybe a house made of snow and ice with gumdrops on the roof and twinkling lights hanging from the rafters. But this looks like any normal but comfortable log cabin on Earth. There are big squishy armchairs in front of the fire, a little rustic dining table with two chairs, and tucked away in one corner, a small work bench and a big, red tool chest.

"Is that where you make all the toys?" I say, half joking.

"Yes."

My head spins. It's all so much humbler than the movies portray. It looks more like Geppetto's workshop than Santa's. How many hours must he sit there, hunched over, making toys for so many children. No wonder he only makes them for the very best kids. The rest of us just aren't worth it.

"Where do you keep them all? All the toys, I mean."

He offers me his hand. "Would you like a tour?"

How can I say no? Horniness pushed aside for a second, I follow him as he shows me the sights. He starts small with the kitchen and bathroom, and his big, comfortable looking bed covered in thick red comforters.

But when he leads me down a spiral staircase into the basement, I'm hit with the knowledge that his life is something far grander than I can comprehend. The storage space beneath his house stretches on forever in all directions.

"It's empty now," he tells me, as though I can't see that. "Before Christmas Eve this entire place was packed with toys. I don't know how many. It took so long to get them out."

"How do you make them? With Santa magic?"

He smiles proudly. "Quite a lot of Santa magic, yes. But I make each one individually. It takes a lot of time."

"I'll bet."

Our lives are so, so completely different. I work on a reception desk, while he labors away over his little workbench. And goodness only knows how many days' work he does just in the time I'm on my lunch break. Guilt surges through me as I try to figure out how much time he has wasted with me, when he should have been here, working, making gifts for those who deserve them.

Will people wake up disappointed next Christmas because I was sucking Santa's dick on my couch?

"Why?" I ask. "Why do you do all this? What do you get from it?"

He breathes in slowly through his nose. "Happiness," he says at last. "It makes me happy to imagine the children waking up on Christmas morning. Their smiles."

It's another punch to the gut, but I can't blame him for it. He doesn't know how badly it hurt to be left off his list every year. "Do you have any children of your own?"

He shakes his head and smiles. "No, it's just me here. And you, for as long as you want to stay."

Right now, I feel like I could happily stay forever. Just Claus and I on Planet Santa, fucking for all eternity. It's tempting, but I know he has to get back to work. And I have a life to get back to. A simple, boring, human life, without polar bear monsters or magic. Or him. It hurts just to think about.

"Would you come with me a moment? I want to see if I can show you something else."

Sometimes the way he phrases things confuses me, but I'm just a puny human and he's... well, you know. I just smile and nod, taking his hand as he leads me back up the stairs to his quaint little living room. He can keep showing me things for now, no matter how insignificant it makes me feel. At least while this lasts, I still have an excuse to stay.

We head out of the back door, our feet crunching on the frozen blue grass. Now that I've been inside, the icy wind hits me, knocking the air from my lungs in a spiraling plume. Claus wraps his arm around my shoulders and pulls me to him.

"I could make you a thicker coat," he offers. "One which makes you feel like my arm is always around you."

Tempting, but I know there will come a time when that sensation would bring a bitter sting of longing. I force a smile. I don't want him to see how tangled my emotions are right now. "I prefer the real thing."

A delighted smile plumps his cheeks.

We arrive at a large barn, and he lets go of me for a second to pry open the heavy wooden doors. Even with his seemingly limitless strength and power, the doors hesitate to let him in. But when they give way and I see what the barn contains, my heart lunges.

Santa's sleigh is like every picture I've ever seen of it. Huge and red, with ornate gold decorative carvings. And though I never believed in him as a child, a thrill of wonder travels through my body and makes tears pool in my eyes.

"Claus…" I whisper, my voice trembling. "It's your sleigh."

"You can see it?"

I reach out and press my hand to the red painted wood. My palm tingles, and a crackling energy raises the hairs on the back of my neck. I close my eyes and gasp.

"Do you feel it?" He asks. I swear there's a little tremble in his voice.

"It's… is that magic?"

Claus nods but his eyes are drawn to me, not the wondrous, fantastical vehicle filling half of the barn. "Normally humans can't even see the sleigh, much less touch it and feel the magic ingrained in it. Perhaps spending time with me has attuned you to it, or, more likely, you're just wonderful."

Okay, there's every chance he's bullshitting me, but right now I feel so fricking special.

Eat my ass, all other humans.

My chest swells a little with pride as I turn to face him. I have the undivided attention of his midnight blue gaze

"Is this how you feel all the time? All tingly and breathless." I ask.

"Not all the time," he says. "Just when I'm with you."

I want you, I think, as loud as I can. I want you, and I need you. I wish you would kiss me. I want you to fuck me. My breath hitches as he steps toward me.

"I'm picking up some hints," he says with a wry little smile.

My stomach flutters. "Good. You can act on them, if you want to."

"I want to."

With one big, strong hand he reaches out and brushes my hair back, starting at my temple, down over the arc of my ear. I shiver, a combination of his magic, and the pure, unchecked human need coursing through my body.

I melt into his kiss, giving myself over to the heat of his lips, his tongue against mine, his hands in my hair, holding me to him. I'm all too aware I can't stay here forever, and he can't come to earth and use up his precious moments when he should be making toys, but we can make the most of now. If nothing else, I can make sure that Christmas doesn't just come once this year. Or even just a couple of times.

"Can we do it in the sleigh?" I ask, gasping for breath as his teeth nip at my neck.

A whoosh of air rushes past me, and when I open my eyes, we're higher up. We're in the sleigh, him in the driver's seat, and me in the passenger side.

And Claus is no longer kissing me. He sits back, his thick thighs parted wide, the bulge of his erection straining against the denim of his jeans.

"Tell me what you want," I say, letting my hand follow the curve of his cheek. "You're always giving me what I want, but what about you? What does Claus want?"

His dark eyebrows raise a little as his lips part. Has anyone ever asked him that before?

"I want…" He stops himself, his lips clamping shut around a half-finished thought. His brow furrows deeper. "Would you take off your clothes? Slowly. The human way."

I can't help but smirk a little. Nothing gives me confidence like knowing this man, this millennia-old being wants me naked more than anything else. He could have anything. He could conjure his every desire from thin air, but he wants me. Slowly, I stand and unzip my coat.

"Anything you ask," I say.

Next, I lift my green sweater over my head. It should be cold, but the combination of magic emanating both from Claus, the sleigh, and my own lust-fueled body heat, keeps me warm.

I keep my bra on and unzip my jeans, wiggling out of them and trying my best to retain at least a shred of sexiness while trying to escape the tight ankle cuffs. There isn't a whole lot of space at the front of the sleigh, but Claus doesn't seem to mind.

His eyes are fixed on my breasts, watching them jiggle and spill over the top of my red lace bra.

He bites into his lower lip. "Holly…"

A thought bubbles up inside of me, pushing against the barrier of common decency blockading my throat. If I'm doing this, I may as well go all the way. It isn't enough that I'm standing in my underwear on Santa's sleigh. But it isn't enough yet. I want it all. I want…

"The suit?" He asks, arching his eyebrow.

"Yeah." Heat spreads across my cheeks as I look down, ashamed. "I know. It's weird, isn't it?"

Claus chuckles quietly. "Yes. But if there's anyone across the two dimensions who I want to get weird with, it's you, Holly."

I raise my eyes, and my pussy damn near lunges for him. He's still sitting, legs splayed wide. His cock is straining hard against his pants, but now they're bright red velvet, tucked into huge black boots. The bright red jacket is wide open, displaying his silver chest hair and the soft, round hill of his belly.

My fingers flex with the urge to touch him. I want to fuck him so hard he remembers me for a thousand years. I want him to feel the same sense of wonder I do when I look at him. A deep, longing sigh emerges from him.

"Take off your underwear," he tells me. "Let me see you."

I'm breathless as I unhook my bra and let it fall down to join the rest of my clothes. Claus reaches into his pants and begins to slowly stroke his hard cock. We seem to be alternating requests, so I guess it's only fair I ask him for something I want.

But as I pull down my underwear, he seems to get the idea. He produces a red foil packet and opens it carefully, before rolling a candy-striped condom over his erection.

I bite my lip and grin. "Nice."

"I thought you would appreciate the festive touch."

I can't tell him my feelings toward Christmas are at best complicated. That Christmas is still easily the worst time of my life, and yet this, with him, this is incredible.

"Come here," he tells me, and I'm only too happy to follow his lead.

I sidestep over to the driver's side and stand between those thick, juicy thighs, bending at the waist to kiss him. The soft red velvet and fluffy white trim of his jacket brush against my nipples as my lips tug at his, my hands exploring the hills and valleys of his magnificent body. As our kiss deepens, he places his hands on my hips, and gently urges me around until I'm facing the front of the sleigh.

"Oh, reverse cowgirl?" I ask, glancing over my shoulder.

He simply urges me down, spreading my ass cheeks so he can watch himself enter my pussy. My spine tingles as I sink onto him, gripping the front of the sleigh. "Ffffuck."

It seems impossible now that I would forget this sensation in just a few hours. I remember him feeling good, but not like this.

He fills me up, as his big hands reach around to cup my breasts and pinch my nipples. My breath emerges in desperate, heavy bursts as I lean back against him, the curve of his belly fitting against my back. His teeth sink into my shoulder as he stifles a moan.

"Holly," he whispers, and then a word in his own language which sounds very close to "Liebchen."

Whatever he says, his meaning is clear. It's a term of endearment, and one which sounds so lovely and tender, my stomach flips at the sound of it.

A moan escapes my lips as I grind my hips against him, loving the way he feels and the way he makes me feel. Loving everything about him. And as his hand travels down over my stomach, and his fingers begin to circle my clit I realize, I'm dangerously close to loving him.

But I can't let that happen. I can't lose my heart to someone I can't have a life with.

Curling my fist around a leather strap lying across my palm, I suck in a breath. A team of eight reindeer are now harnessed to the sleigh and I'm holding their reins.

"Hold on tight," he whispers.

And with a thrust of his hips, I feel like I'm flying.

Because I am.

CHAPTER TEN

Two days ago, if you'd told me I would be riding Santa's sleigh and his dick at the same time, I'd have laughed in your face. But here I am.

We soar, higher and higher into the clouds as the reindeer gallop through the air. The rush of sensation is overwhelming; the icy air tearing past us, the hot, thick cock filling my pussy, the tenacious fingers strumming my clit, the warm mouth on the back of my neck. Excitement sharpened with just a zesty hint of fear, makes my heart pound. But I know Claus won't let anything happen to me.

The reindeer seem to know what they're doing, so I concentrate all my attention on Claus, on this feeling. I lift my hips and sink back down onto him, sending wave after wave of pleasure rolling through my body. It seems to be working on him too.

"Holly…"

"Oh, fuck, Claus," I moan as he starts to draw firm circles with his fingertips, bringing me closer and closer to the edge of orgasm. The soft plush texture of velvet brushes the back of my thighs, and beneath that the firm warmth of his big, strong thighs.

I press back against him, tilting my head so I can kiss him again, lost in the sensation of his eager lips, the gentle tickle of his pristine white beard. He pinches my nipple with his left hand, as his right moves harder, faster, as though there's nothing in the universe more important to him than my pleasure.

I cry out as I come, hard, my body tensing, my pussy gripping his cock. I ride him throughout, bouncing on his lap as his deep, broken moans give me goosebumps.

And then I'm standing, leaning forward, my feet on the wooden floor of the sleigh, bent over the guard rail as he thrusts into me from behind, over and over, harder, deeper. Frost blue plains and snow-capped mountains blur beneath me as I cling on for dear life. He pounds into me with ferocious desperation, his fingers digging into my hips, pulling me back to him whenever he withdraws.

My heart shatters as I realize this is the last time. This is our last time.

As send offs go it's pretty fucking fantastic, but still, as he gives one last powerful thrust and his feral cry breaks through the rush of the wind, I can't stop a tear from falling down my cheek.

"Holly?" His voice wavers as he withdraws from me completely and turns me around to face him. Sapphire eyes search my face. Magical eyes I might never get to see again.

"I'm sorry," I whisper, wiping the tear on the heel of my hand. "God, what's wrong with me?"

"Nothing, you're perfect." He shakes his head, but his eyes remain wide and desperate. "Did I hurt you? Did I do something wrong?"

"No. Not at all. It was amazing."

He raises his hand to swipe another tear from my cheek with the rough pad of his thumb. I catch his hand in mine and hold on to it, pulling it to my chest. I don't even know when we landed, or how we find ourselves back in the big barn. I certainly don't remember being wrapped in a big, fluffy white blanket, but as I pull it tight around me, covering my naked body, I know I must have needed it. The reindeers have gone, and the icy air no longer whips around us. It's just Claus and I.

He sits back. The red suit is gone, transformed into his creamy knitted sweater and thigh-hugging jeans. He opens his arms wide to welcome me into his embrace.

"I have to go back to my world," I say as I climb onto his lap and wrap the blanket around him too. Nothing can come between us in the woollen cocoon, at least for a little while. "I can't stay here forever."

"I know," he says sadly.

We sit together, holding each other. The heavy thud of his heart beats against my ear as my fingers tangle in the fuzz of his beard. He's so comforting, yet forbidden.

"I'm sorry I stopped believing in you," I say.

He sighs a little and shakes his head. "Every human does. They have to, or I'd never be able to make enough gifts. Don't apologize for it."

I have a lot to apologize for. Almost all my life, there has been a weight on my chest. I've been slowly suffocating, weighed down by the curse of guilt.

I never much believed in curses, but if the past couple of days has taught me anything, it's that impossible, magical things exist. I may as well try to lift it. In fairytales, evil magic is often broken by kisses, or by heartfelt words.

The kisses haven't helped, so pulling in a deep breath, I speak my mind. "I stopped believing because you didn't bring me the one thing I wanted."

Pressing my lips together, I close my eyes. Silence stretches the moments as he waits patiently for my elaboration.

"Holly," he says gently. "Is there something you want to talk to me about?"

"I think I have to."

He nods. "What did you wish for? How did I fail you?"

I sniff and lower my gaze. There's no point trying to hide it from him. "I wished for my dad. I wished he could come back to life."

Beneath the silky white hair of his beard and moustache his lips are downturned as if he already knows what happened. Maybe he does but he needs me to tell him.

So I do.

"He loved Christmas, with all his heart. The whole family did. His name was Douglas, like the fir tree." I drag in a breath. "I was four years old, almost five when he took me to the Christmas tree lot to help pick one out. It was the first Christmas I was really aware of what was going on, you know?"

Claus nods, but he doesn't speak. He just holds me and lets me carry on."

"I guess I didn't like the cold or didn't get my own way or something, but I had a tantrum, a huge one." A hot tear rolls down my cheek. I don't even know when I started to cry. "Dad was trying to get me back to the car while carrying a tree on his shoulder and... I'm not sure what happened. I got away from him and he chased after me, and there was a car. He didn't see it coming and—"

I can't go on, and I don't need to. Claus' arms tighten around me. His big hands gently stroke my hair as silent tears track down my cheeks, and I breathe in the soothing warmth of his body.

"Holly…" He whispers against me. "I'm so sorry."

"I hurt so many people that day."

"You were a child."

"A child who killed her dad."

"Holly, no."

"I did. I know I did something terrible, something unforgivable and evil, because you didn't come to me. You never came to my house at Christmas, because you only visit good children."

I feel ridiculous and overly dramatic, but every word of it is the truth. I've carried it in my heart for thirty years, and the pressure has built to the point I can no longer contain it.

"Claus, I hate Christmas. I hate how we're expected to be happy and jolly and grateful. We have to plaster on smiles just for one day so everyone can pretend the world isn't completely cruel and shit. But it is, and Christmas is cruel too, because if you do something wrong at Christmas, if you dare to ruin that special day, you can never be forgiven for it."

He lets me finish, and then he sits there, holding me, letting me rest my cheek against his chest as I spew hatred for everything he works for. Slowly, my breathing returns to its normal rate, and my skin begins to cool.

Claus inhales slowly. "You didn't kill your father, Holly, he died."

"That's what everyone says."

"And they're right."

The heat of him pressing his lips to the top of my head gives me a little comfort as I listen to the beat of his heart.

"Secondly, I don't believe there's any such thing as a bad child," he says. "Children are simply reacting to their world and the obstacles it throws at them. Sometimes they do bad things, but that doesn't mean they are bad. And I certainly would never see a four-year-old girl whose father had just died and think she was bad and didn't deserve toys. That's not who I am."

There's nothing but kindness and concern in his eyes, and it hurts me worse than if he'd confirmed my lifelong conviction that it was all my fault.

"Then why didn't you come?"

"I don't know," he says softly, his voice rumbling against my ear. "I can't possibly remember every child, so I can't tell you exactly what happened. Sometimes children get missed, or they move home and I don't realize. Sometimes addresses get mixed up. If they didn't, we never would have met."

A prickle of embarrassment heats my face. That Christmas, Mom and I had gone to stay with Aunt Ivy so they could try to reassemble the fragments of our family into something recognizable. Was it just that simple? "But you're Santa Claus. You're supposed to know everything."

"I'm a toymaker, Holly. I'm good, and I can do a lot, but I'm not omnipotent. There are billions of children on earth, and I've been doing this alone for a very long time. I can only leave toys for the children who desperately want them and truly believe in me, regardless of goodness or badness. If they need toys and a little magic, I can do that."

I close my eyes as the truth settles around me. Everyone in my life has been telling me the same thing for thirty years. Everyone except myself. I'd become so convinced of my guilt I'd sentenced myself to a life of penance.

But I was just a child. A four-year-old doing what little children do.

"You never came to my house because I didn't believe in you."

"Please know that even if you did, I could never have brought your father back to you. Even if I didn't make a single toy for a thousand years and concentrated all my skill and attention to it, I can't do that. I can't stop death. After…" He breathes in deeply, bracing himself. "After Mary died, I blamed myself too. I spent a lot of time torturing myself, telling myself I could have done something, somehow halted the passage of time."

A kick of empathy jolts my heart. "I'm sorry."

"It was a long time ago, and she's at peace."

"How did…" I stop myself from asking. "I'm sorry."

He smiles softly. "It's okay, I can talk about it. She had a long, happy life here with me. Longer than humans are ever supposed to live. She died quietly, and comfortably. But Holly, I still blamed myself. And perhaps that's just one more reason our hearts are drawn to each other. Our lives may be completely different, but we've both known that pain."

I close my eyes as he presses his lips to my forehead, stroking back my hair. If I stayed here, he would likely have to watch me grow old and die too.

"Liebchen, if I could have anything for Christmas, it would be for you to know that you aren't to blame for what happened." Claus pulls back to look at me. "I can promise you with all my heart that the reason I didn't bring back your father all those years ago wasn't because you were evil or unworthy of forgiveness. Because I know you better than I know any human on earth and I know your heart is good. So wonderfully and beautifully good."

I shake my head, but my spirit is already lifting at his words. "We hardly know each other. It's been two days…"

"You knew me the moment you laid eyes on me. And I know that you are the type of person whose heart aches at the thought of someone else being sad, and who doesn't want anyone to get hurt, even if they are a giant bear monster."

The corner of my lips quirks a little. "You think I'm a good person?"

"I know you are. One of the very best," He smiles. "The kindest, the sweetest... Unless, of course, there is an intruder in your home," he clasps my chin in his fingers and raises my face so he can look me in the eye. "Then you'll run them through with a sword, but, well... goodness is a spectrum."

I can't help but laugh, and in turn his body shakes with a chuckle.

At the sound of my laughter a glint of hope glitters in his eyes. "You know, I heard your mother's wish when she came to your house and she saw me."

Of course he did. Instinctively, I brace myself for impact, already certain that the answer involves the one thing we can't ever have. "What was it?"

"Your happiness," he says plainly. "She wished that you were happy and that you would forgive yourself."

A lump swells inside my throat. I have to look away from him so I don't cry again, because deep down I know he's right about everything.

Claus hugs me tighter. "Your mother also wished that she could find herself a man like that. The rest of it I can't tell you."

I swat at him, and earn myself another chuckle.

"Wait, can you do that?" I ask. "Can you help her find someone?"

"No one can control the course of love. But it is technically still Christmastime, and your world still clings to a little magic. Who knows what will happen?"

I love when he talks like that, all mystical and otherworldly. A shiver travels along my spine. It becomes hard for me to breathe, but it's a pleasant, giddy sensation, one I never want to end. But it does. Every second which passes is another one we'll never get back. I know our supply of stolen moments is running short.

"I'm going to miss you," I say quietly, tracing a finger down the valley in the center of his chest, until his heart beat pulses against my palm. It can't be much later than noon in my time, but I'm exhausted. Between our heavy conversation, the warmth and comfort of being held by him, and, of course, all the orgasms, I'm tuckered out. "Do you think it would be okay for me to sleep here? Just a nap."

"Of course."

I'm all mushy and heavy, my eyelids refusing to open. "I don't want to go back out to the cold. Can you zap me to bed?"

The next thing I know I'm sinking into a warm mattress, being covered by thick, soft sheets. The gentle crackle of a log fire breaks the silence and the air smells of gingerbread and pinecones. I want him to lie down next to me and hold me, but I remain alone.

"Sleep as long as you like, Liebchen," Claus says gently beside me. He strokes back my hair as I roll onto my side. "I have to go out, but I'll be back as soon as I can, and then I'll hold you."

"Okay," I murmur. I'm curious, but I can't summon the energy to question where he's going.

As I sink into the warmth and comfort of his bed, I listen carefully until I'm sure he's gone.

Only when I'm alone do I say the words I've been too afraid to admit even to myself. "I think I love you."

CHAPTER ELEVEN

I yawn and stretch beneath the blanket, rubbing my eyes until I can focus on the thick wooden rafters crisscrossing above me. It has been a long time since I slept so deeply and felt so refreshed. The fire is still crackling away so I can't have been asleep long. I must have really needed that nap.

The world feels clearer somehow, and my breaths come easier than they have done for… well… ever.

Rolling onto my side, my heart lifts at the sight of the man sleeping beside me. Claus is peaceful, his features smooth and serene. He must have used magic to get into bed because I certainly didn't feel him moving around. He sleeps in nothing but his boxers, and it takes every ounce of my self-control not to reach out and touch him. I don't want to disturb him.

Instead, Claus shifts, edging his way toward me until our bodies are pressed together, wrapping me up in his arms and resting his chin on the top of my head. We fit together so perfectly.

How is this my life? How am I lying in bed in another dimension, cuddled up to Santa Claus? And even weirder, I'm desperate to find some way to make this work between us.

"Good morning," he mutters without ever opening his eyes.

I breathe in the scent of him and sigh. "Where did you go?"

He murmurs sleepily before yawning, his big body stretching and pressing against me as I wait. "To your home," he says.

Home. I feel nauseous when I think of it. Home to my quiet little house, my desk job, my sad, grey little life. I have to leave him, even if I keep putting it off. Maybe we can make it work just spending the dregs of Christmas Eve together… but it wouldn't be enough. Deep down, I know I need more than one night a year.

"Why?" I ask.

Claus strokes my hair, his touch soothing yet firm. "Do you remember, when you came home on Christmas Day, there were two boxes?"

Of course I remember. I remember the candy-cane striped clit-sucking device, the magical ribbons tying me to the bed. I'd felt naughty, and I couldn't wait to tear into that bright red package.

But I'd completely forgotten about the second box. "The nice box."

One edge of his lips quirks up a little. "I brought it here for you, if you want to open it."

"I do."

It sits on the bed between us, pristine white and tied with gold ribbon.

My pulse kicks up a notch at the sight of it. I sit up in the bed. "What's in there?"

He chuckles, propping himself up on his elbow beside me. "Open it."

My mind races as I tug open the bow on top. Maybe it's something sexy but not quite so wicked as the toy he made me. Whatever it is, my fingers shake as I lift the lid from the box and look down on… another box.

Claus grins.

"Mean," I whisper, but I'm smiling.

It's unmistakably a jewelry box, about three inches cubed and a pale, shimmering blue inlaid with silver on the corners and the embossed letter H on the top. It's especially for me.

"Thank you." I'm already a little watery-eyed as I pick it up.

"You haven't opened it yet."

"I know." I move the white box out of the way and shuffle closer to him, snuggling against his chest. "Just, thank you."

"You're quite welcome, Holly. Always."

I lift the lid and the blue box opens smoothly, revealing a sparkling silver necklace. The chain is made from the tiniest, most delicate loops I've ever seen. It feels more like a strand of silk than metal, and I'm nervous just touching it. In the center of the necklace, hangs a miniature glass snow globe.

And inside the globe is a tiny, perfectly lifelike building.

"Is that...?"

"Your house, yes." Claus smiles as my eyes rake across his handsome features.

"How did you make this? It looks exactly like the real thing."

His smile turns boyish, filled with wonder and delight. "It is the real thing."

"I..." My mouth opens and closes a few times as my brain struggles to put the pieces together. "What?"

"With this necklace, you can travel between our dimensions in an instant." Claus sits up and takes it from the box. "All you have to do is shake it, and tell it where you want to go. If you're here and you want to go home, just tell it. If you're home and ever want to come back..."

"I can come back?"

"Whenever you want to." Claus's arms surround me as he kisses the back of my neck. "If you want to."

"I do. God, Claus of course I do."

My breath stutters as he lifts the necklace over my head and places it around my neck. It hangs low enough that I can see it against my chest. There's even a tiny puff of smoke coming from my chimney, and though at first glance it looks completely still, the longer I stare the more I realize that it is moving very, very slowly.

"I can't spend much time in your world. I have too much to do before next Christmas and I wouldn't have enough time there," Claus says. "But this way we can still see each other often."

"But time moves so differently here. Won't you be alone most of the time?"

Claus lays back so I follow him, snuggling beside him and resting my head on his chest. The slow beat of his heart pulses against my ear as I skate my fingers through the hair on his stomach.

"You're worth waiting for, Holly."

I swear my heart stops completely at his words. And when the touch of his lips restarts it, it damn near glows. I raise my head and twist my body around so I can face him. The light in my chest sparks a fire, tearing through my veins and heating my blood.

"I want you," I tell him, whispering the words against his lips.

"Again?"

"Always."

He rolls over and opens a drawer on a bedside table, rummaging through balled up pairs of thick, woollen socks.

Eventually, he pulls out a condom and rolls onto his back to put it on. I smile fondly as I lie back and watch him. Sure, he may be thousands of years old, a magical shapeshifter, and possibly an alien or something, but he's still just a man. A loving, kind, sexy man who loves more than anything to make me come.

I couldn't ask for anything more.

With the condom on securely, I pull myself up and straddle his hips, just like I wanted to on Christmas Eve. He props his back and shoulders up on the pillows so we can kiss. As I lower myself onto his cock, I can't help but throw back my head and gasp. He gives me the Kringle tingles like I've never felt before, and nothing in the world has ever felt so indulgently good.

Claus groans, his fingers gripping my hips, clinging to me as though some part of him is still afraid I'll leave and never come back. As though I could ever give this up. As though I could ever find anyone else who makes me feel this way.

Leaning forward, I wrap my arms around his shoulders, languidly rolling my hips to draw both our pleasure out as long as possible. He kisses me, my shoulders, my neck, my breasts, every slow, lingering touch of his lips an act of worship.

There's no magical device that can ever feel this good, nothing supernatural. Just him and me, our bodies and hearts together.

When he comes, his body shivers, and he barely misses a beat before he sits forward and pushes me gently onto my back. I can hardly breathe as he buries his face between my thighs, licking my clit and moaning like he's never tasted anything so good. I come, hard grinding my pussy against his tongue, then pull him back up toward me so I can kiss the taste of me on his lips.

"Holly…" He whispers my name as if I'm someone magical and otherworldly, someone he can't believe is his to hold.

My fingers reach out to touch the soft white plush of his beard, still not quite believing that this is happening.

That I, the woman who has always hated Christmas, am falling in love with Santa Claus.

EPILOGUE

I bolt upright as a clatter downstairs wakes me. The clock at my bedside reads 4 a.m. It's December twenty-fifth, and my heart is backflipping in my chest.

He's here.

I climb out of bed and tiptoe out of my room and along the hallway. The cold winter's night air nips at my bare skin.

I see Claus every day, but Christmas is always kind of special. After all, it's the anniversary of when we first met, five years ago. Five Earth years anyway.

In fact, these days, I'm rarely on Earth. It started out as me shaking the globe every evening, or each time I managed to hide in a closet somewhere at work so I could pop over to his workshop for a quickie.

Eventually, it became less of a treat and more of a habit... okay maybe eventually is the wrong word. I have precisely zero chill when it comes to Claus. It was less than two Earth weeks before I officially moved in with him. But I still come back home for the holidays and the occasional weekend. For us, our time together on Planet Santa feels like months, and what blissful, slutty months they are.

Still, as I tiptoe toward the stairs, my skin prickles with anticipation. Though I see him almost every day, the human realm feels just that little bit more magical when he's here.

I sneak down the stairs quickly, hoping he still has the suit on. I know he can still hear my wishes, so I make them loud and vivid. He'll probably think it's cheesy for me to find him underneath my Christmas tree, me scantily clad in a little sheer red babydoll negligée with white fluffy trims, but so what? I missed out on Christmas for three decades, and now I have the best Christmases of anyone.

"You know, you don't get presents if you aren't asleep," his deep voice purrs from the living room.

I peer around the edge of the door, before leaning against the frame seductively. "You are my present."

"Oh, is that so?" He quirks an eyebrow and sets his big, brown sack on the floor by the fireplace. He's playing Mr. Cool, but I can tell he likes the babydoll. His eyes trail along the length of my figure, his chest heaving as he pulls in a breath. "Well, I suppose I'd better send all these back then."

"Hm. It's probably for the best. I have been very naughty this year."

"Not at all," Claus groans a little as he sits on the couch, his legs spread wide. He holds out a hand and gestures for me to come to him. I don't need to be asked twice. "You are always exceptionally nice."

I straddle his hips, kissing him as he strokes a feathery touch along my sides. His lips taste of soot and the cold night air. He has a far-off, weary kind of look, his eyelids half-drawn.

"Tired?"

"Very," he whispers, barely able to keep his eyes open. "But I'm also desperate to have you."

"You do have me, always. I'll want you just as badly when you wake up." I push my hands up beneath the hem of his coat, relishing the warm, fuzzy softness of his stomach as I kiss him again. He's making a valiant effort to stay awake, but I know from experience he'll be in a deep sleep within minutes. Two billion cookies and glasses of milk will take their toll on a guy.

I wrap my arms tight around him and shake the little snow globe on the end of the chain, wishing we were back on Planet Santa. Claus barely reacts as our bed materializes instantly beneath us, and he sinks back into the plump white pillows.

"I love you," he murmurs.

"I love you too," I reply, the words as easy as breath.

He cuddles closer to me, pulling me against his big, warm body. I breathe in the scent of him, the chimney smoke, the leather and frost. We can head back to Earth later, once he has recouped his strength. We can still be there in plenty of time for dinner at mom's. It's her first Christmas with her new guy, so this year feels extra special.

But before that I want to tire Claus out all over again… and maybe again after dinner too. And possibly for dessert.

He chuckles softly, keeping his eyes closed. "Anything you want, as many times as you want, since it's Christmas."

I can't help but smile. Best holiday ever.

THE END

ACKNOWLEDGEMENTS

Thank you to Jake for reading this as I wrote it and giving me the confidence to go on even when I was worried no one would want it. Also thank you for remaining married to me while I simp for Santa Claus.

Thank you to all my lovely patrons over on Patreon, with special thanks to the Vixens For Life, Emily H, LB F, Katie B, Melanie, Linda W, Janel A, Deanna S, and Amanda F. Your support means the world to me and I couldn't have done this without you.

Thank you to Ali for your help with formatting.

Thank you to Santa Claus for being hot and for not suing me. I believe in you.

And thank you so much to you for reading this, for taking a chance on my weird little book. I hope you have a very *very* nice Christmas but stay firmly on the naughty list.

ABOUT MARIE LIPSCOMB

Marie specializes in writing romances with plus sized heroines and plus sized heroes. She is the author of the **Hearts of Blackmere** and **Vixens Rock** series as Marie Lipscomb, and also writes short, bonkers, high-heat romances including **No Getting Ogre You** under the penname M.L. Eliza.

Originally from Bolton, UK, Marie now lives in North Carolina, USA, with her husband, Jacob, her dog, Alfie, Jacob's dog, Belle, her fish named Fishfish, and Merlin the bearded dragon. When she's not writing, she can usually be found playing the same three video games on a loop (*cough* Dragon Age).

Printed in Great Britain
by Amazon